Child Bride

ALSO BY CHING YEUNG RUSSELL

Moon Festival
Lichee Tree
Water Ghost
First Apple
A Day on a Shrimp Boat

Child Bride

by
Ching Yeung Russell

Decorations by Jonathan T. Russell

BOYDS MILLS PRESS

Special thanks to my editor, Karen Klockner

—C.Y.R.

Text copyright © 1999 by Christina Ching Yeung Russell
Illustrations copyright © 1999 by Boyds Mills Press
All rights reserved
Published by Caroline House
Boyds Mills Press, Inc.
A Highlights Company
815 Church Street
Honesdale, Pennsylvania 18431
Printed in the United States of America

Publisher Cataloging-in-Publication Data

Russell, Ching Yeung.
Child bride / by Ching Yeung Russell ; decorations by Jonathan Russell.—1st edition.
[xxx]p. : ill. ; cm.
Summary: An eleven-year-old Chinese girl is sent to her grandmother's village for an arranged
marriage, and tries every method she can think of to escape her fate.
ISBN 1-56397-748-6
1. Marriage customs and rites—Fiction—Juvenile literature. 2. China—Social life and customs—Juvenile fiction. [1. Marriage customs and rites—Fiction. 2. China—Social life and customs—Fiction.] I. Russell, Jonathan, ill. II. Title.
[F] —dc21 1999 CIP
Library of Congress Catalog Card Number 98-73070

First edition, 1999
The text of this book is set in Gilliard
1 3 5 7 9 10 8 6 4 2

To my mother
and sisters, Lily Kam and Rita Nishimura,
for their constant encouragement,
and
in memory of my Uncle Seven, Chan Sing,
who provided a wealth of information for this book.

—C.Y.R.

Author's Note

One year when I went to see my paternal grandmother, Ah Mah, for the New Year greeting, she said, almost mumbling to herself, "I wonder if I should find you a home." I didn't understand why she said that. She knew I was living with my Ah Pau, my mother's mother. But I didn't ask her to explain, because my relationship with my Ah Mah was not close. We were like strangers to each other. She always asked me routine questions: "What grade are you in now?" and "Do you make good grades?" I felt very timid and awkward, sitting with my legs together and my back straight. Most of the time, I stayed no more than half an hour, using the excuse of having a long journey, and said good-bye. I hurriedly left her house and headed back to Ah Pau's home, which would take about half a day of walking between the rice paddies.

Later on, when I grew up, I realized that the home Ah Mah was thinking of was a husband's home—which was in her mind a girl's permanent home. That gave me the inspiration to write this book. Most Chinese parents worry whether their sons can produce a son to carry on the family name and whether their daughters will marry and have a permanent home. I guess my Ah Mah said what she did because my parents lived far away and she felt responsible for my future.

The child bride-to-be in this book was drawn from the combined stories of my aunt, my cousin, my friend, and myself. My aunt—my father's sister-in-law—was a child bride. She is about ninety years old today. Her family was very rich, and she had land and jewelry as a dowry when she married my uncle. She slept in the same bed as my Ah Mah until she was eighteen. In the early years of the Chinese Republic, in the 1920s and 1930s, it was still very popular in our area to marry a young girl. The girls were around twelve or thirteen and were called "little brides."

One of my cousins ran away to Hong Kong after her mother arranged an engagement for her. It was in the mid-1950s. The whole village was stirred up because no one living there had ever run away from a marriage before.

A childhood friend of mine got pregnant by a married man when she was eighteen. Her father was furious because the family's reputation was ruined. Even though it was in the mid-1960s, he found her a husband, a rice farmer from a rural area. The farmer arrived, rowing a sampan on his wedding day, but my friend had disappeared. She had run away to Canton to avoid marrying the farmer, who was a stranger to her. The news of the stood-up groom demanding his bride spread throughout Tai Kong.

Long ago, the process of making a marriage match was taken very seriously in China. The parents looked at the bride's and groom's birth times and dates. They checked both families to make sure there were no deformities or serious disease three generations back. The bride and groom had to be matched in their social levels. Of course, appearance was very important, too, for both husband and wife.

When I met my future husband, the first thing my mother asked was for me to bring him home and let them see him. (In judging a man, the first impression is formed by looking at his nose, in judging a woman, it is by looking at her mouth.) Later, Mother and Uncle agreed that Phil looked strong and honest. He had a tall, straight nose. I actually had a red mole under my nose above my lip and received compliments about it until it disappeared when I was in my mid-twenties. When I was in high school and first fell in love with a schoolmate, his mother and relatives forbade him to date me because I was tall and slim. They feared that I was not strong enough; they wanted to find someone more plump-looking. They also said that I had coarse hair, which was believed to denote stubbornness and an unwillingness to obey. Their criticism left me with emotional scars for a long time.

In the old times in our area, the search for a daughter-in-law was quite interesting. If a family thought a girl looked like she would make her husband die young, they wouldn't choose her. If a girl's mouth was too big, they feared that she would make her husband poor all his life. I actually had a friend whose maid remained single because, according to my friend, the girl's mouth was too big. She worked as a maid until she passed away. Being chosen as somebody's bride long ago was considered a lucky accomplishment for a girl's parents.

I talked recently with my aunt, who was a child bride, about her wedding. The ceremony was kept very simple, except for offering tea, because she was just a little girl. However, customs and procedures for weddings vary even among the Cantonese. In Tai Kong, for a regular wedding, the bride's family would send little cakes to their relatives and friends along with the wedding invitation cards. The bride's friends, so-called "sisters," would accompany the bride to the groom's house, then the sisters would return home.

The dowry was carried to the groom's home on the day of the wedding, if not earlier. The more expensive the bride's dowry, the more she would have "face" and be respected in the new home. The bride, who had a red cloth covering her whole face, would cry all the way until she reached the groom's home. When the bride got to the groom's house by sedan chair, the groom either used a folded fan or a bamboo stick to hit the sedan chair's door three times (some just kicked the door) to show his power as a husband. Then the groom took off his groom's hat and tapped it on top of the bride's head—indicating the bride's need to obey—before the bride was allowed in.

Afterward, the bride and groom offered tea. This was a ceremony that would most likely decide the fate of the bride in her new home. Sometimes the mother-in-law would show authority over the new bride by not taking tea until the bride knelt on the floor for a long time. Sometimes, if the mother-in-law had been mistreated by her mother-in-law when she had first offered tea, she would take revenge on her new daughter-in-law.

The bride would go back to visit her own family with her husband on the third day after the wedding. It was the day for the groom to meet the bride's family officially. It was also the day when the bride's family was anxious to see if the groom would bring a whole roast pig as a present, which indicated that the bride had been a virgin before the wedding night.

Years ago the "little bride" would share a bed with her mother-in-law or sleep alone until she was older, and she would not have returned to her home after three days.

Today the practice of arranging marriages for "child brides" is all but abandoned. Many other traditional wedding practices have also disappeared or been simplified, although a number of Chinese parents and grandparents retain some of the old ways of thinking. They still consider the family background and personal appearance of the bride and groom important, but they are not always given a lot of say by the bride and groom.

In *Child Bride*, I have told the story of a young girl who is caught between two sides of her family—one side which is wealthy and expects her to follow traditional wedding customs, and one side which is poor. It is her strong tie to her grandmother on the poorer side of the family that gives her the courage to rebel against the wishes of her wealthier grandmother.

—C.Y.R.

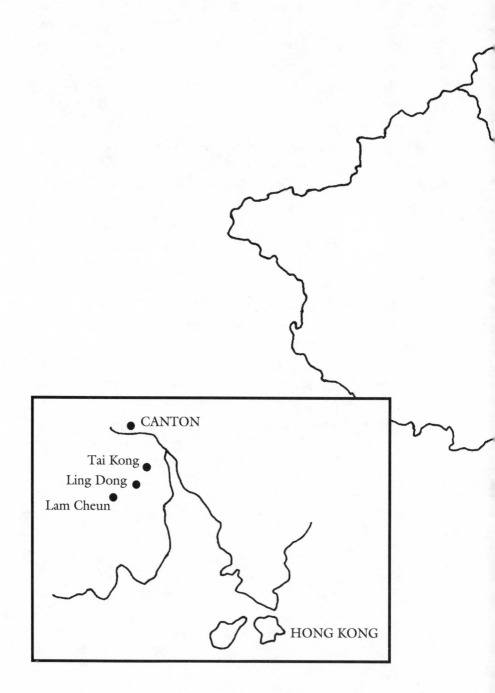

MONGOLIA

KOREA

CHINA

BEIJING ●

SHANGHAI ●

CANTON ●

● TAIWAN

● HONG KONG

Tai
Kong

Chapter 1

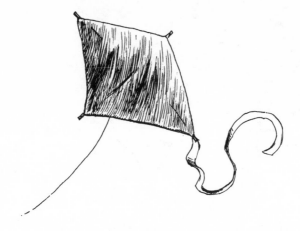

It was early April. A brilliant azure sky stretched above us, dotted by only a few wispy white clouds, as we prepared to fly our kite on top of Ford Hill. I called out to my cousin Ah Mei, who was holding the long-tailed red kite about twenty feet from me, "Let's go!" Ah Mei was twelve, a year older than me, but shorter.

Holding the spool of string in my right hand, I ran away from her, looking back at the same time. Our kite quickly rose up into the sky on the spring breeze. The kite made a *flip flip* sound as the gentle wind filled out its diamond shape and drew it heavenward.

"Give it more slack," Ah Mei commanded. I held the spool between my hands and let the string unwind completely. The kite soared upward, like a red sailboat, gliding leisurely against the blue sky. I felt myself being pulled by the kite, so I leaned back, letting my weight hold me against its tug. The kite sailed over our Chan Village, two rows of gray brick houses standing next to one another in the shape of a horseshoe. It sailed over our small town, Tai Kong, which was located about seventy-five miles southeast of Canton. It sailed over the silvery, serpentine branch of the Pearl River that flowed around Tai Kong and Ford Hill, like a cat's tail curling around its master's leg.

I was feeling very proud of my navigational skill when Ah Mei said, "It's my turn, Ying!"

"Wait," I said without taking my eyes off the kite.

About ten minutes later, Ah Mei said again, "My turn now."

I reluctantly handed her the spool. In a few seconds, I cried, "Pull! Pull! Hard! Run! Run! Oh . . ."

The kite, as if hauled down by a sudden gust of wind, dropped and disappeared over the edge of a peak. I ran toward the spot where the kite had fallen while Ah Mei quickly reeled in the string. We found our kite tangled in a pine tree, with the cord still loosely connected to the spool.

We tried to retrieve it by jumping, but it was too high. We didn't want somebody else to get the kite. As we were trying to find a long stick, Ah Mei pointed to a flat, grassy clearing down below us and asked, "Hey, is that Wong Chi? Ask him if he can help us."

I looked in that direction. There were two young men sitting on the grass, talking leisurely. One was Wong Chi, my cousin Ah Won's third cousin. The other person I hadn't seen before. Since Ah Mei was shyer than I was, I raised my voice and shouted, "Hey, Wong Chi, can you help us get our kite?"

The two young men turned and looked at us. "Sure," Wong Chi said. He stood up. The other man, who was wearing a white shirt and gray trousers, followed Wong Chi as he climbed the hill to where we were standing.

Wong Chi said, "We saw a kite in the sky, but we didn't know it was yours." He jumped several times, but he couldn't reach it, either.

"Be careful! Try not to break the string," I said.

The other man, who was taller, jumped but also had no luck. Finally he suggested that Wong Chi climb on his shoulders. With the added height, they were able to retrieve our kite.

Ah Mei thanked them, but we couldn't fly the kite anymore because the tail was ripped and needed to be mended.

"Do you come here very often to fly kites?" asked Wong Chi's friend.

"Yes. It's very close to Chan Village," I said.

"Oh, you are Chans," he said.

"She is," Wong Chi said, pointing to Ah Mei. Then he looked at me and said, "She isn't."

"My name is Yeung Ying. I live with my mother's mother, my Ah Pau."

"I see," the man said. I thanked them as Ah Mei continued to reel in the string.

Ah Mei whispered to me as they were ready to leave,

"Ask who the other man is."

"Hey, who is your friend, Wong Chi? We haven't seen him before."

"Oh, his name is Lo Sing. We studied together in high school. But now he goes to college in Canton."

Lo Sing nodded, then smiled.

Ah Mei's eyes followed their departure while I folded the kite's torn tail. Then we went back to the village.

When I got back home, lunch was already on the table, but I didn't see Ah Pau.

"Ah Pau!"

No answer. As I approached the table, I saw Ah Pau lying on the daybed. Her eyes were closed and her mouth was wide open, but I couldn't see her chest moving up and down. I put my ear on her chest, but I couldn't hear her heart beating, either. My own heart seemed to fly out of me. I embraced Ah Pau's body crying, "Ah Pau! Ah Pau!"

Ah Pau awoke, startled by my hysteria. "What's wrong?"

"I thought you were dead," I cried. "I couldn't see you breathing at all."

"Dai gut lai see!" Ah Pau said.

"How come I didn't see you breathing?"

"Sometimes it's hard to notice older people's breathing when they are asleep."

I was glad that Ah Pau was okay. I knew she had been feeling very tired recently. The left side of her back was bothering her, too. To reassure me, she said she probably just strained her back without even knowing it. "As long as I don't irritate it, the pain will go away soon," she told me. So I was not as concerned about her back as I was about her tiredness.

I helped her get up for lunch. We had egg custard steamed with chopped-up fish intestines—our favorite—along with a small dish of salty turnips and another one of cooked lettuce in clear broth. But Ah Pau ate only a couple of bites of the egg custard and put her chopsticks down.

"Are you full already, Ah Pau?"

"I don't feel like eating."

"Let me see." I immediately put my hand on her forehead, like she did when I had lost my appetite. Then I put my hand on my own forehead. It didn't feel any different.

Ah Pau stated, "I'll be all right. Maybe the weather has affected my appetite."

I didn't insist on Ah Pau eating because sometimes I didn't feel like eating, either. But I didn't want anything to happen to my Ah Pau. Even though I was living with her and Uncle and Auntie and their family, Ah Pau was the one who took care of me ever since my parents left to work in Hong Kong six years ago. I didn't know what I would do without her. I had to take care of her the way she had always taken care of me. I was grown up now—eleven years old. Ah Pau was very old—she was seventy-three.

Chapter 2

Ah Pau loved to eat duck. Late the next afternoon, I went with Ah Mei to the rice paddies at the foot of Buddhist Hill, on the outskirts of Tai Kong, to catch fiddler crabs. I wanted to fatten up our ducklings, which Ah Pau had bought last month at the farmers' market. Even before we got to the rice paddies, we could see hundreds of acres of tender green rice plants rustling like an ocean, waving in the breeze. As we got closer, we could smell the strong odors of cow manure and rich soil. I inhaled deeply. I loved that familiar smell.

Ah Mei and I walked down a narrow dirt path between the paddies, where the roots of the rice plants were all submerged in water. The irrigation ditches, which were about ten feet wide, lay between the paddies, but did not have much water in them. The mud banks of the ditches were full of holes—the homes of the fiddler crabs. After we reached our special place, we rolled up our tattered pants and stepped into the slimy, oozy mud.

All at once the crabs, about one inch wide, scurried for their lives. I spotted a huge, red-clawed creature about two feet away from me, waiting alertly by its hole as if to challenge me. As I approached, the crab shot into its hole. I couldn't move as fast as it could, because my feet sank into the mud, up to three or four inches above my ankles. Each step became a struggle. Every time I lifted a foot, the hole would fill immediately with brownish water, and I looked as if I were wearing a muddy rubber boot!

But I didn't take my gaze away from the crab's hole. I used my spade to turn the hole inside out and expose the crab. Then quickly, I put my left hand on its dark gray shell to stop it from running away. The crab frantically waved its two red claws in the air. I dropped the spade and gripped the sides of the shell with my right hand, picking it up carefully to avoid its claws. Bubbles started forming around its mouth, like water boiling in a rice pot. I studied the bubbles getting bigger and bigger for a few seconds before dumping the crab into the basket I carried on my back. I was always fascinated by these bubbles, but I didn't understand where they came from. None of my friends knew, either. The crab didn't give up; it frantically scratched at the basket, trying to get free. But the long-necked basket was designed to prevent the crabs from escaping.

I began to chase another one. *"Aiyah!"* I lost my balance while pulling my foot out of the mud and fell backwards right into the slime! Ah Mei, who was standing behind me, laughed out loud. Then she carefully helped me up. My bottom felt sticky and very uncomfortable. But I went back to work. After I had caught about thirty crabs, I decided to quit. I was so muddy and still felt uncomfortable. The sky wasn't dark yet.

On the way home, we washed ourselves as best we could in the pond next to our school. We couldn't wait to get home to take a real bath because the mud had dried and made us feel very itchy.

Just as we stepped into the Chan Village plaza, Ah Won and a few small children saw us and said to two ladies, "There she is." The plaza was a long, open space between the two rows of houses. The ladies stood talking in front of our house.

One of the ladies was Mrs. Tong, a middle-aged rich woman. I had spoken with her for the first time about a month earlier. The other lady looked a little like Mrs. Tong, but was younger and heavier.

"They are looking for you," Ah Won said, carrying her baby sister on her back with a *meh dai*. Ah Won was ten. Her black hair was cut in the shape of half a coconut shell. Aside from being my cousins, she and Ah Mei were also my best friends.

I approached the ladies and asked Mrs. Tong if I could help her. She said they had just wanted to say hello to me. I felt embarrassed because of my patched clothes, and I was sure my hair still had small pieces of dried mud in it.

I heard Mrs. Tong, whose front teeth were all capped in gold, whisper to the other lady, "See, on the right side."

From then on, the other lady's eyes didn't leave my face. She seemed to be very interested in me. She asked, "Do you miss your Ah Mah?"

Before I could tell her that I didn't miss Ah Mah—my father's mother—because I hadn't seen her in years, Mrs. Tong said, "This is my younger sister. Do you remember I told you I had a sister who lives in Ling Dong, around Lam Cheun where your Ah Mah lives?"

"Yes, I remember," I replied.

"I'm sure your Ah Mah would like to see you," Mrs. Tong's sister said, taking my dirty hand.

I felt very uncomfortable with the way she held my hand and the way she looked at me. *Did Ah Mah send her to see me?* I wondered. I didn't ask, but I wished Ah Pau were here. How could I entertain these ladies? I asked Ah Won if Ah Pau was home. She said Ah Pau had gone to the pond to call the ducks back home. When I told the ladies Ah Pau should be back soon, Mrs. Tong said they needed to be leaving.

After they were gone, Ah Mei said, "I think they came here just to see your red mole! Maybe I am wrong, but they seemed to make such a big deal over it."

"Really?" I said. I had a tiny red mole on the right side of my upper lip. People always mistook it for a mosquito bite. Mrs. Tong had commented on it once before and told me it was lucky.

"When they left, I heard the sister say that you are a little skinny," Ah Won said. "Maybe your Ah Mah asked Mrs. Tong's sister to visit you."

"It could be," I said. "But why wouldn't they say so?"

"I don't know," said Ah Won.

Ah Mei and I returned to our houses. I went into my back courtyard, put the spade and basket on the ground, and got ready for a hot bath. Ah Pau was home and had already heated a pot of hot water for me. When I came out of the bathhouse, she had encircled the ducklings with a chicken fence in the corner of the courtyard. She had also boiled the fiddler crabs in a steaming pot. The crabs had turned bright orange. I couldn't help myself. I picked up the biggest one, pulled off the legs and the shell, and stuck the whole crab into my mouth. I chewed and swallowed it quickly even though it was hot. I was so hungry and I loved that special fishy crab taste. Ah Pau was ready to chop up the rest of the crabs for the ducklings, but I told her I could do it later.

"How do you feel, Ah Pau?"

"I feel better today."

"Good. Let's eat. I'm starving." I helped Ah Pau bring the food from the kitchen to the table in the living room.

While we were eating, I told Ah Pau about Mrs. Tong and her sister. I also told her what Ah Mei and Ah Won had said—that the ladies seemed so interested in my red mole, and had said I was a little skinny.

Ah Pau dropped her bowl on the table. Her face turned pale.

I jumped up and hugged her. "What's wrong, Ah Pau?"

"I'm okay," she said, picking up her bowl as if she had just recovered from a nightmare.

But I knew something wasn't right because Ah Pau didn't finish her supper. Instead, she knelt in front of the worship table the rest of the evening.

I stared in the mirror at my red mole, but I couldn't figure out why Ah Pau was behaving so oddly.

Chapter 3

About ten days later, Ah Pau's condition hadn't improved. She went to see the herbal doctor in town and took herbal tea for a few days. Sometimes she seemed to feel a little better. But I could tell that she was still tired and her appetite hadn't improved. I told her I was going to write to Uncle, who was working in Canton. But she stopped me, saying that it would make Uncle worry unnecessarily.

I tried to stay home as much as I could to help with household chores like brewing the herbal tea, washing clothes, tending the ducklings and chickens, and cleaning out the chamber pots. But it didn't help Ah Pau's health.

I noticed that her eyes were not as vivid and sharp as before. They looked dull. Her body seemed much smaller and her face looked gaunt, like her skin was stretched around her skull. Her appearance worried me.

I wished Auntie and Kee, my thirteen-year-old cousin, would return home. They had left about a month and a half earlier. Auntie's mother was celebrating her eighty-first birthday, and Auntie wanted to spend some time with her. Kee went along to accompany his mother because his Ah Pau lived way beyond Canton. Kee's teachers had given him the homework assignments, and Auntie's mother planned to hire a private teacher. Auntie and Kee would be back in another month or so.

I knew Ah Pau's health would not improve, even if I quit school, did all the work, and spent every minute with her. I felt restless. I couldn't stand watching Ah Pau become weaker and weaker every day. I knew deep down that she needed medical treatment, not just herbal tea. Finally, I decided to write to Uncle behind Ah Pau's back. I remembered Uncle's address in Canton by heart. I knew Ah Pau would be furious if she found out, but I had to do it, no matter what.

The next day in school, I wrote a short letter to Uncle and used my own savings for a stamp. After I dropped the letter into the mailbox on the main street, Tai Gai, I felt terrible. I thought I was betraying Ah Pau, who had never done anything behind my back!

I shuffled home, disheartened. I wanted to go home quickly to be with her, but I was afraid to face her.

On the way home, I saw two boys carrying a billboard

on their shoulders. Together they were shouting: "Kung Fu show! Kung Fu show! This evening at Leung's Plaza!"

Ah Pau loved to watch Kung Fu shows. To avoid thinking about the letter, I ran into our front courtyard, calling to Ah Pau, "There's going to be a Kung Fu show . . . ." But I stopped suddenly.

Sitting with Ah Pau was an old lady I didn't know who had big, thick lips. She was sipping tea, sitting on a tall stool across the table from Ah Pau. Ah Pau looked very upset. I felt my heart skip a beat: I was sure the old lady had already told Ah Pau what I had done. Before Ah Pau could blame me, I hastily greeted her without looking at her or asking her how she felt, and was ready to climb up to my room in the attic to hide.

"This is Ah Choi. Your Ah Mah sent her here."

I stopped, feeling relieved. I hadn't been caught. But what a coincidence that Ah Mah's name had been mentioned again. While I was wondering why Ah Mah had sent Ah Choi here, Ah Pau said, "Ah Choi is going to spend the night here." She didn't tell the visitor my name, though; it was as if the lady already knew me.

Ah Choi, who looked a little younger than Ah Pau, was wearing a coarse black *tong cheong sam*. She kept sipping her tea and staring at me over the rim of her teacup. She didn't give me a normal greeting, like a guest who hadn't met me before or hadn't seen me for a long time would have.

Her staring made me uncomfortable. Ah Pau said to me, "You go to the pond and get the ducks back." It was just a little after three o'clock, a couple of hours earlier than the usual time for calling them back. I sensed that Ah Pau didn't want me there. Perhaps she and Ah Choi had some secret?

I put my book bag in the attic and left for the pond. As I went out the door, I heard Ah Pau say to Ah Choi in a kind of worried tone, "She hasn't even dropped the red yet." What did she mean? Is that what Ah Pau was worried about?

During supper, Ah Pau was very quiet. I checked with her several times, but she always said she was okay.

But I knew something was not right. I felt sure it had something to do with Ah Choi's visit and their secret talk. I wondered if Ah Choi was a matchmaker. I remembered the year before, when a matchmaker had come for my eighteen-year-old cousin Ah So. The matchmaker had wanted Ah So to be a concubine to the town bully. But then I laughed. No one in our house needed a matchmaker. I was too young, and Ah Pau was too old!

Almost immediately after supper, Ah Choi went to sleep on my bed in the attic. I would sleep on Kee's bed in the living room. Right after I helped Ah Pau with the dishes, Ah Pau said she wanted to talk to me. She told me to sit next to her on the daybed and declared, without looking into my eyes, "Ying, your Ah Mah is very sick."

"Oh? That's what is upsetting you?"

She didn't answer me but simply said, "She sent Ah Choi to take you to Lam Cheun to see her."

"Why? Why do I have to go? I hardly know my Ah Mah."

"Even though you hardly know her, she knows you. You are her granddaughter."

"I don't want to go. You are not feeling well, and I don't want to leave you."

"I'll be all right. Don't worry."

"I don't want to miss school. Midterm exams will be coming soon." I made as many excuses as I could think of. In fact, my mid-term exams and not knowing much about Ah Mah were not the main reasons—Ah Pau was my main concern. I didn't want to leave her while she wasn't feeling well.

"Your Ah Mah wants to see you before she dies!" Ah Pau's voice was harsher all of a sudden. I knew from experience that something was bothering her. But she tried to soften her voice, "I can't say no to your Ah Mah. I am only your mother's mother; she is your father's mother. From the top of your head to the bottom of your feet, you belong to the Yeung family. I can't do anything to prevent you from going there or stop her from doing something that I don't agree with. I can't say no. I must obey. Do you understand?" Ah Pau looked like she was about to cry.

"What is it that you don't agree with?" I asked.

"I mean . . . I just mean that I don't want you to go, but I don't have any choice. You are only my maternal grand-daughter. I cannot change anything."

I knew that even though I had lived with Ah Pau and her family for several years, by tradition I still belonged to the Yeungs. My father's family had authority over me, not the Chans. I didn't want Ah Mah to be angry with Ah Pau, so I said, "I understand, Ah Pau. I'll just go to see her and then come right back."

I thought Ah Pau would be happy to hear that I had changed my mind, but she wasn't. I was a little disappointed, because I had only agreed for her sake. I would do anything for her.

Ah Pau pressed my shoulders for a long time as if she had something more to tell me, but she didn't. Instead, she sobbed.

"Why are you crying, Ah Pau? Ah Mah will not be mad at you if I go to see her."

Ah Pau dabbed her eyes with her sleeves.

"When do I leave?" I finally asked.

"Early tomorrow morning."

"That soon? How can I tell my teacher?"

"I can tell her."

"Where is Lam Cheun located, anyway?"

"It is just a little south of here."

"Is it a big town?"

"No, it is smaller than Tai Kong—only a few streets, and no electricity at all. Most of the people around there are poor rice farmers."

"Is she a rice farmer, too?"

"No. Your great-great-grandfather was some kind of officer in the Ching Dynasty. Your Ah Mah also came from a rich family and is an educated woman."

"Oh. How long will it take us to get there?"

"About one whole day. You have to start before dawn."

"*Whaah!* It will take two days to go back and forth, even if I don't stay?"

"Sometimes you have to do things you don't want to do. It's part of life."

I remembered the way Ah Choi had stared at me.

"But should I trust Ah Choi on such a long journey? I hardly know her," I whispered.

"You don't need to worry about her. She has been your Ah Mah's servant since your Ah Mah was a little girl."

"How could that be!"

"Well, Ah Choi was sold by her family to be your Ah Mah's servant. When your Ah Mah got married, she took Ah Choi with her because Ah Choi is considered your Ah Mah's property, even to this day. So, Ah Choi has been working for your Ah Mah for many decades. She's very loyal to your Ah Mah. You can trust her."

"I'll try. How do you know all this?"

"I was originally from Lam Cheun before I married your grandfather—your Kung Kung—remember?"

What Ah Pau said eased my mind about Ah Choi. I went to bed immediately after Ah Pau said she would help me pack.

Chapter 4

Ah Pau woke me up way before dawn. She and Ah Choi had already cooked rice, salted duck eggs, and dried salted fish. But I couldn't eat. I wasn't used to getting up that early.

"You have to put as much as you can into your stomach because you don't know when you will have a chance to eat," Ah Pau said. So I ate a half bowl of rice.

Ah Pau's eyes didn't leave my face while I ate. She acted strangely, like she didn't recognize me at all.

After I was through eating, Ah Pau handed me a dark green *tong cheong sam* and said, "I finally finished altering this to your size from Ah So's old clothes last night."

"Didn't you go to bed?"

"Yes, but I went to sleep late. I don't want you to look so poor in front of your Ah Mah."

I put it on and it fit me perfectly, even the pants, which usually were too big when I got new clothes. Ah Pau always made my clothes with room for me to grow; she said that way I could wear them for a long time.

"Thank you very much, Ah Pau."

She nodded. "I put ten *yuan* in the pocket."

"Ten *yuan*! What am I going to do with it?"

"When you're on a journey, Ying, money is very important."

"One *yuan* is plenty, Ah Pau. You should keep the ten *yuan* for yourself to see a doctor."

"I have money. Don't worry."

She handed me a large bundle wrapped with a big black kerchief.

"How come it is so big?" I asked, untying it to see. It looked as if *all* my clothes were there, including my cotton jacket! "I will only be gone for a few days, not for a year, Ah Pau!" I said.

Ah Pau was speechless for a few seconds. Then she said, "It's always better to take some extra clothes when you're away from home. Don't ask too many questions. Here." She handed me a small, long-handled, woven basket. It smelled of warm sweet potatoes. "In case you are hungry on the journey," she said.

I told Ah Pau that she didn't need to go to the ferry with us. She looked exhausted and kept massaging the left side of her back. But she came anyway.

Outside, it was still not dawn, and no one was on the

street. Ah Pau gave me instructions as we walked, "Remember to be polite, and talk softly. Otherwise, your Ah Mah will think that I didn't teach you any manners. Most important, be sure to eat enough and don't go hungry. And if you feel chilled, put on more clothes so you won't catch cold. Remember?"

"You sound like I'll be spending the rest of my life there, Ah Pau. I'll be back within a week, and the weather will still be the same!"

Ah Pau didn't say anything until we got to the ferry. The steamboat that ran back and forth from Canton was not there, but the river was dotted with dim moving lights like fireflies. Farmers were rowing their sampans full of fresh produce toward the warehouses along River Front Road. Ah Choi led us toward a pier that was not far from the landing. A big, well-lit passenger sampan, about twice the size of a normal one, was docked there. A canopy made of woven split bamboo covered part of the boat. Two boatmen were waiting at either end. Each of them held a long bamboo pole that came up out of the water. They looked like they were ready to cast off.

When we reached the end of the pier, Ah Pau suddenly seized my arm, as if she didn't want to let it go. "Don't forget to eat more and don't catch cold," she repeated. Then she started to cry.

"Ah Pau, I'll be right back. Please don't cry." But my eyes were clouding with tears. I wiped them away with the back of my hand. She began crying even harder and held onto my arm even more tightly, as if our separation were a matter of life and death, until Ah Choi parted us, saying, "She'll be all right."

I wanted to comfort Ah Pau longer, but Ah Choi grabbed my hand and urged me to get into the sampan. "We have to start now; it'll be dark when we arrive at your Ah Mah's house."

There were no other passengers in the sampan. Underneath the canopy was a clean bamboo mat with two neatly folded blankets and two pillows. As Ah Choi and I stepped in, the sampan wobbled a little, then steadied itself. Just as I put my belongings on the mat, Ah Pau, who was still sobbing, bent down to get a better look at me and said, "Take care of yourself, Ying."

"I will, Ah Pau. Don't cry. I'll be back soon!" I waved at her.

The boatman in the front untied the rope. Then he pushed the boat away with the bamboo pole. The boat gradually left the pier and glided toward the middle of the river, then headed south. Ah Pau's frail figure remained at the end of the pier. She was waving and wiping her tears at the same time. I made my way closer to the front of the sampan so I could be nearer to her. "Ah Pau, go home!" I yelled as loudly as I could. Suddenly, I began to think of Ah Pau having to go back all by herself to the empty house, where there would be no one to take care of her, no one to help her wash clothes, and no one to empty the chamber pot for her. My tears began to flow. I put my hands to my mouth like a megaphone and shouted, "Ah Pau, go home! Be careful on the pier! Take care, don't eat any fried food. Ah Pau . . ."

"Come back," Ah Choi said to me, but I didn't pay any attention to her. I kept yelling, "Ah Pau! Go home! I'll come home soon! Ah Pau, don't cry. Eat more and rest. Ah Pau, don't cry." I yelled until Ah Pau's small, stooped figure was entirely out of sight. It was only then that it dawned on me that this was the first time in my life I had ever left my Ah Pau.

Chapter 5

It was also the first time that I had sailed on that kind of sampan. I was so seasick, I felt as if I were dying. I threw up all my breakfast on the deck. Ah Choi helped me clean up the mess I had made. The rest of the day I didn't eat, for fear that I would get sick again. I gave Ah Choi my food. Most of the time I was thinking about Ah Pau and wondering about her appetite. It occurred to me that I should have asked Ah Mei's mother to check on her for me, but it was too late for that now. I should have thought about it earlier. But I was glad that I would be back to Ah Pau within a few days.

When we got to Lam Cheun, the sun was going down. I was thrilled to be on land again. The river was quiet and narrow, much narrower than the one in Tai Kong.

We were the only boat to dock. The riverbank seemed to be deserted—no warehouses, no farmers, just some trees scattered along the edge. But a burgundy sedan chair was stationed next to a big banyan tree near the small landing. I thought I misunderstood when Ah Choi told me to get in, because I had never ridden in a sedan chair before.

"We have to hurry," Ah Choi said.

I got in with my belongings and my basket, which had only one sweet potato left, and tried to make room for Ah Choi. As I was waiting for Ah Choi to get in, two bearers came over from behind the banyan tree. Without any warning, both of them picked up the sedan chair with a jerk, and my head bumped into the back of the chair.

"Ah Choi, you're not coming?" I asked, poking my head out of the opening in the front of the chair.

"She can't sit inside!" the bearer in the front turned and shouted at me. He had a big, ugly white scar about two inches long above his right eyebrow. I didn't dare to ask Ah Choi why she walked beside the sedan chair instead of riding with me. I was afraid the man with the scar would yell at me again.

There were no other pedestrians. The narrow dirt path was bordered with sugarcane plants that were as tall as a man. I had always been afraid of walking next to sugarcane fields. They seemed spooky, and I had heard that people who had leprosy lived there. I wished Ah Choi would just sit next to me instead of falling far behind. I closed my eyes to avoid looking at the fields.

I fell asleep. Suddenly I heard someone shout, "Go

away! We've no food to give you!" I opened my eyes and glimpsed the back of a child with long, stringy brownish hair disappearing around the corner of a big house. Then the sedan chair was lowered roughly, and I almost fell forward. In front of me was a huge, spectacular house. Now, the faded memory began coming back to me. A red lacquered plaque with two black carved characters that said YEUNG FAMILY hung over the massive red doors.

I was so taken aback by the splendor of the house that I didn't know what to think. It was much more magnificent than I recalled. And now, for the first time since we began the journey, I started to wonder what Ah Mah looked like. Did she have a lot of wrinkles like Ah Pau? Did she have teeth missing in the front? Would she be happy to see me, or was she so sick that she would barely open her eyes to see her poor granddaughter? What should I say to her when we met?

Ah Choi finally caught up with us. She opened the two heavy red doors and told me to come in. A large, clean courtyard, almost as big as Ah Pau's whole house, lay before me. There was a porch made of square clay tiles on the right side of the courtyard. A high wall of folding wooden panels, all carved with designs of bamboo, birds, and flowers marked the entrance to the main house. Above the panels was an intricate fretwork to let in the gentle breezes.

"Follow me to the outhouse," Ah Choi said as she led me to the door at the far end of the courtyard. It opened onto the kitchen. The kitchen looked as big as Ah Pau's whole living room. We went through the kitchen to another exit, which led to a back courtyard paved with granite. A plump gray cat was lying curled up at the threshold of the kitchen door.

A high brick wall, which had shards of broken glass along the top to prevent thieves from climbing in, surrounded the courtyard.

A gnarled old banyan tree, which I vaguely remembered, stood at the middle of the back courtyard, shading almost the whole area. One of the big limbs stretched out over the wall. The outhouse and bathhouse were behind a brick storage room. Nearby was a door leading into the street.

Ah Choi helped me prepare water for a bath. She poured hot water from an insulated jar into a large basin, and then drew water from the well on the other side of the courtyard. She poured the cold water into the hot water, checking it with her hand. Once the bath was ready, Ah Choi went back to the kitchen, and I began to bathe. Pretty soon, tantalizing cooking odors made me feel very hungry.

After the bath, I felt relaxed and fresh. I changed my underwear, but put on the same clothes, and wore my wooden clogs. Ah Choi returned and told me to go to the living room to meet my Ah Mah.

The living room was dim inside, and I had to let my eyes adjust to the dark. On the left were two tea tables and a daybed. On the right were two carved recliners with a tea table between them, holding an elegant bonsai. In the middle of the room was a round, carved table, topped with marble, and four chairs. A worship table stood at the far end of the room. All the furniture was made from *seen ji*, the finest quality wood available, carved in the same dragon-and-phoenix pattern, much fancier than Ah Pau's old beat-up furniture. No one was in the living room. I thought Ah Mah must be so sick that she was still in bed.

Ah Choi set up a big kerosene lamp in the middle of the marble table. Then she returned with food. I started to help Ah Choi, but a stern voice came from the corner, "You're not supposed to make such noise!"

I quickly searched in the direction from which the voice came. There I discovered a small lady, dressed in black, sitting at the right side of the worship table, with her back facing the wall. She seemed to be holding a Buddhist rosary. I assumed that the lady must be my Ah Mah, whose face I had forgotten. Then I began to think, *Ah Mah was supposed to be very sick and about to die.*

"Your clogs. . . . Act like a lady!"

I realized that I wasn't holding my clogs tightly to my feet when I walked, and they clonked on the floor. "I'm sorry," I mumbled.

I was afraid to move and kept swallowing nervously. I hadn't had anything in my stomach since early morning, and I felt as if I could eat all the food on the table myself. After what seemed a long time, the old lady finally got up from the worship table and shuffled in an awkward gait toward me. I remembered that kind of walk. Looking down, I noticed the tiny, embroidered, pointed shoes. She had bound feet, a fact I had completely forgotten.

"Ah Mah," I greeted her timidly.

"Uh," she said. She was a little smaller than Ah Pau, but her appearance was much more delicate. Instead of the coarse clothes Ah Pau wore, Ah Mah wore the fine fabrics of the rich. Her shiny, neat hair, fixed in a bun, was not as gray as Ah Pau's and was held in place by a jade clasp. She wore a pair of apple-green jade earrings and a jade bangle. She looked like a wealthy, high-class lady compared to Ah Pau, who was a poor peasant.

"Sit and eat," she ordered. Her eyes were sharp and bright, as though she could see through me into my heart.

I cautiously walked to the round marble-topped table and sat down.

Ah Choi helped Ah Mah sit next to me, but Ah Choi did not sit down. She just stood behind us. I wondered why Ah Choi was not eating with us.

I did as Ah Mah told me. I picked up the ivory chopsticks, which were more splendid than Ah Pau's plain bamboo ones. There were three serving dishes. The most attractive to me was the whole fish steamed with silklike slivers of ginger root and green onions. And the big head, my favorite part of the whole fish, was pointing right toward me. That was mine to eat, for sure. There was also broccoli, stir-fried with small pieces of boneless chicken, and a bowl of black mushroom and pork soup. It looked like a reunion meal on New Year's Eve. How I wished Ah Pau were here to share the food!

I was hungry enough to devour all of it, but I couldn't start because I had to wait for Ah Mah to begin. She acted as if she was not interested in the food. Finally, she picked up her blue-and-white porcelain spoon and prepared to eat soup right out of the serving bowl, but then she stopped and remarked, "Keep your legs together when you're sitting down."

I was stunned. She must have noticed my legs when she sat down.

"I'm sorry," I mumbled.

Ah Mah dipped some of the soup with the spoon, and then said, "Now you can begin."

"Thank you," I replied. I put down the chopsticks and picked up my spoon. Before I could reach for the soup, she stopped me and asked, "Did your Ah Pau never teach you any manners?"

I looked at her, puzzled. Her sharp, bright eyes were fixed on my face, as if she were inspecting me. "You never say anything before you eat at your Ah Pau's house?"

"No . . . Oh, yes! Please eat, Ah Mah."

"You can eat now."

I picked up my spoon again and scooped up some soup. I was so hungry, I put the whole spoon inside my mouth.

"You should sip the soup like a young lady does, and straighten your back!"

"Yes, Ah Mah," I whispered, sitting up straight.

She picked up her bowl and chopsticks and gracefully raked a small amount of rice into her mouth. I did the same. How I wished that she would quickly eat all the fish meat so I could get the head!

After she swallowed her rice, she instructed me, "Never open your mouth while you're chewing your food."

"Yes, Ah Mah."

"And never say anything until you have swallowed all of your food. Your Ah Pau didn't teach you any manners at all."

I felt injustice in her comment about Ah Pau. It seemed as if Ah Mah was trying to find fault with anything and everything I did. Why was she so harsh? Wasn't she happy to see me? I wished I hadn't come at all. I swallowed the rice with great difficulty. The fish head, which Kee and I always fought for at home, lost all its appeal. I wanted to leave the table, leave this house. For the rest of the meal, I was very cautious. I picked up whatever Ah Mah picked up to eat. Unfortunately, her bowl was only half full, and she was soon finished with the meal. I followed suit, putting the chopsticks neatly aside, even though I was still hungry. Ah Mah said, "Eat more. You're skinny and pale."

I wondered if I really could.

Ah Choi at once took my empty rice bowl from me, refilled it, and gave it back to me. I felt funny about her serving me.

I ate cautiously, trying not to open my mouth, even though it was awfully hard to chew food that way. I nervously finished the second bowl of rice. I could have eaten another bowl and finished all the food, but I didn't. I preferred to eat my last sweet potato in private, without anybody looking at me or judging my ways.

Ah Mah stopped me from helping Ah Choi with the dishes. I felt uncomfortable just sitting there. But someone knocked at the door. Ah Mah immediately warned me, "Anything you need, just ask me or Ah Choi."

"Yes, Ah Mah," I replied, wondering why she had said that.

Neither Ah Choi nor Ah Mah went out to open the door. I said, "I'll open it."

"Sit down!" Ah Mah said harshly.

Chapter 6

I was extremely curious about who was at the door. When Ah Choi finally opened it, a lady dressed in attractive light-gray clothes appeared in front of us. She looked very tired and upset. When she saw me, she cried with delight, "Oh, Ying, you have grown up like a little princess! Do you remember me?"

I didn't have any idea who she was. She looked like she was much younger than Ah Choi, perhaps in her thirties. Instead of having a braid in the back like other women her age, her hair was cut short, with little waves. I turned to Ah Mah, who was back at the worship table, for help. But she was doing her prayers. Ah Choi had just walked away. I said timidly, "I don't know . . . ."

"Oh, I am your Auntie Three. I had just married your

Uncle Three when you were born. You were like a little dried-up shrimp! You cried so hard that your mother got tired of holding you, so I cuddled you in my arms and you went back to sleep. Now I just can't believe you have grown up so big and pretty like a princess! Last time I saw you, you were this short," she said, indicating about two feet with her hands.

I liked her at once, not because she said I looked like a little princess, but because she was friendly. I liked her even more when she mentioned my mother, whom I barely remembered. I felt instantly close to her because she had known my ma.

"Wait, let me go to my room," she said, rushing off. In a few minutes, she returned with a piece of material in her hand.

She unfolded it. It was a small piece of white satin with small green and red flowers scattered all over. Then she held it up in front of me.

"See, now you look like a *real* princess! It's much better than that material you have on—that makes you look like a country girl!"

I wanted to tell her that Ah Pau stayed up almost all night to fix my clothes, but I didn't.

She continued, "I'm going to ask the tailor to make you a new outfit. I can use the leftover fabric to make beautiful ribbons for your braids, too."

"Will you really do that?" I asked, thrilled, because I had always envied a rich girl in my class who had colorful ribbons for her braids. Her ribbons always looked like two beautiful butterflies.

"Sure I will. Tomorrow I'll make them for my little princess!"

Ah Mah hobbled in front of me and said, "Follow me."

I saw Auntie Three casually throw the material on the stool next to her, looking angry, but she didn't say a word. I dared not say anything to my aunt, so I picked up my belongings and followed Ah Mah. She led me into the middle bedroom, where a kerosene lamp was hung on the wall. There was more furniture in that room than in Ah Pau's whole house. Ah Mah pointed to the bed on the left side of the room, where a mosquito net was already hanging down, ready for someone to sleep.

"This is your bed. Have a good rest tonight. You have to get up early."

"Thank you, Ah Mah."

I wanted to ask her how she felt and give her Ah Pau's regards. But Ah Mah didn't give me a chance. "Don't talk to anybody but me and Ah Choi," she said as she hobbled off.

I stood in the room alone for a while. Then I went to the outhouse and got ready for bed.

The sky had turned shades of pink and purple. The gray cat had just finished its supper and was licking itself beside a brown dish, where a little rice still remained. When I went back to my room, I was very tired, but I couldn't sleep in the fancy bed. I thought about Ah Pau, wondering how lonely she must have felt when she returned home all by herself. I was convinced that Ah Mah was not as sick as I had been told. Why did Ah Pau say to me that Ah Mah was very sick? Ah Pau had never lied to me before.

Suddenly, I heard a lady yelling and a child crying out in pain. I listened carefully. The sounds were coming from the back courtyard. I got up from the bed and went to the living room, where Ah Choi was helping Ah Mah get up from the recliner. Ah Mah told me, "Go see what is happening."

I ran to the back courtyard, which was dim because the sun had already set. Auntie Three was just closing the back courtyard door and had a broom in her hand, looking like she could kill someone.

"What happened?" I asked.

"That wild child! Look." She pointed to the cat dish. I bent down to have a close look. The dish was full of rice. *Ah Choi must have fed the cat again*, I thought. No wonder the cat was so fat!

By that time, Ah Choi came out, assisting Ah Mah with one hand and holding a kerosene lamp in the other.

"That wild child was lucky this time. I only hit him on the head with the broom handle!"

Ah Mah commanded, "Get the lock and put it on the courtyard door."

"I will," Ah Choi replied.

Auntie Three said, "I don't think a lock can keep him away. That kind of wild child has ways of getting in. Tomorrow I'm going to get some *seh yeuk* and mix it with the rice. If he eats that, he will be as sick as a dog. I don't think he'll dare to return!"

Ah Mah didn't say a word, but waved her hand at Ah

Choi, signaling she wanted to go back inside. Ah Choi seemed disturbed. I followed them, but couldn't help wondering who the wild child was. I felt sorry that he had to steal the cat's food to eat.

Chapter 7

It seemed like I had just fallen asleep when I was awakened by someone. It was Ah Choi. She had already lit the kerosene lamp, filled the washbasin with water, and placed it on the washstand next to my bed. I felt a little funny. I was not used to being served by someone unless I was sick. Rubbing my eyes I said, "You don't need to get water for me. I know how to get it from the well."

Ah Choi ignored me and watched as I washed myself, as if she were afraid that I wouldn't do a good job. Then she told me to sit in front of the dressing table, and moved the kerosene lamp closer. She dabbed white powder all over my face and prepared to shave me with a straight razor. Ah Pau always shaved my face on the New Year, but I was stunned when Ah Choi rubbed rouge on my cheeks after she finished shaving my face. I asked her why, but she didn't answer. About five minutes later, she finished putting on my makeup. I was ready to get up and look in the mirror, but she pushed my shoulders down. "Not yet. We're late."

"Am I going back home?"

She ignored me again and started to comb my hair.

"I can do it myself."

"Don't move," she ordered, sounding impatient. Then she started to comb my hair. I felt as though she were pulling my hair out by the roots. When she had finished brushing, she opened a bottle of hair oil that smelled like roses, sprinkled a few drops into her hand, rubbed her hands together, and worked it into my hair. I liked it. I had never used hair oil before because it was too expensive. Instead of leaving my braids down as I usually did, Ah Choi fixed my hair into two coils on either side of my head and added red silk roses to the middle of the coils.

Before I had a chance to see how I looked with makeup and my new hairstyle, Ah Choi took out a bright red *tong cheong sam* and a pair of embroidered red shoes from the chest of drawers next to the dressing table. There was another rose-red *tong cheong sam* and another pair of shoes in the chest, too.

"*Whaah!* Are those mine?"

"Whose do you think they are?"

"Oh, they are beautiful." I gently touched the material, afraid my rough hands would snag the satiny fabric I had seen only rich girls wear. I never thought I would wear such clothes or own a pair of embroidered shoes!

The outfit was a little big, as were the shoes. But I could hardly tell I had shoes on. The soft, smooth soles felt like cotton!

"Are these from Canton?" I asked. Although Ah Choi was not as friendly as Auntie Three, I was not as frightened to talk to her as I felt with Ah Mah.

"Breakfast is about ready," she said, totally ignoring my question. Then she walked abruptly out of the room.

I held up the kerosene lamp. At last I had a chance to inspect myself in a full-length mirror. It was unbelievable! A strange, bridelike, rich-looking girl was looking back at me. I pirouetted in front of the mirror and felt rich already.

When I came out to the living room, the day was just dawning. Ah Mah and Auntie Three were already sitting at the marble-topped table waiting for me. "Good morning, Ah Mah. Good morning, Auntie Three."

Auntie Three gushed, "Look at the little princess! Come and sit beside me."

I hesitated. But I didn't want to hurt her feelings, so I did. She had on a dark, wine-red silk *keepo*, with a pearl necklace, pearl earrings, and a pearl ring, all set the same way! Her face was rosy. I had never seen such a beautiful, elegant lady in all my life! She even looked younger and prettier than she did the day before.

I sat opposite Ah Mah. She had on a black silk *keepo*. She wore her jade jewelry *and* a matching set of gold jewelry—a necklace with a large dragon-and-phoenix pendant, a pair of gold bangles, and a ring. Her face was not as pale as when I saw her yesterday, and her lips appeared to be red. She had on some makeup, although not as much as Auntie Three. Ah Mah looked anxious.

Ah Choi brought tea and three bowls of steaming hot noodles.

"Ah Mah, eat. Auntie, eat," I entreated them. Then I began to eat carefully, trying to avoid dribbling broth on my new clothes and to keep Ah Mah from correcting me in front of Auntie Three. I looked for an opportunity to inform them that I wanted to return home.

Ah Mah looked very anxious and often asked Ah Choi what time it was.

Just as I put down my chopsticks, Ah Mah ordered me, "Go back to your room and wait."

Wait for what, I wondered. I screwed up my courage and said to her, "I would like to go back home today, Ah Mah."

"Just do what I say."

I was embarrassed at the way Ah Mah ordered me around. Frustrated, I went back to my room, tied up my clothes, and put the basket next to them so I could leave at any minute—as soon as I got Ah Mah's permission. There was nothing for me to do. The flame of the kerosene lamp was burning low. I blew out the light. A smelly wisp of black smoke rose straight from the lamp wick. A beam of daylight shone through a small, high window in the corner of the room. I looked in the mirror again, but my appearance did not excite me as it had earlier. I was upset because I didn't know what I was waiting for, and I didn't like being ordered around by everyone. I didn't like it one bit!

I sat in front of the dressing table, biding my time. I

began to wonder if this was the price to pay for all my new clothes and shoes. I would rather have my own old clothes and be free to do as I pleased.

About ten minutes later, Ah Mah hobbled in awkwardly. Ah Choi followed, carrying a heavy-looking bamboo basket. The top of it was covered with dried *bok choy*. She put the basket down on the floor, removed the *bok choy*, and took out a big jewelry box. She placed it on top of the dresser.

"Have you counted it?" Ah Mah asked Ah Choi.

"Yes. It's okay," Ah Choi replied and then retreated. I didn't have any idea what they were talking about.

"I have to tell you something. I was going to discuss it last night, but you were tired from the long journey," Ah Mah said, sitting on the dressing table bench next to me. She looked even more nervous than before.

"You're a very lucky person. A very, very rich family in this area has chosen you."

I didn't understand.

"Look, everything on this side of the box is your dowry," she said, opening the jewelry box. The gold jewelry and gold bars dazzled my eyes. She picked up an apple-green jade bangle, two gold necklaces with pendants, a small jade-and-gold ring, and several gold rings and said, "This bangle belonged to my younger sister, your great-aunt. It matches the bangle I have on. They were presents from our mother. It is a little too big for you now. The two necklaces and pendants are a gift from me on behalf of your parents. This jade-and-gold ring is Ah Choi's present to you. One of the small gold rings is from Auntie Three, and the other three rings are from other relatives. You have to wear all these pieces for your wedding. The jewelry on the other side of the box is your bride price. You'll have two hundred and fifty acres of rice paddies. You won't ever need to worry about being hungry. And you will also have your own lifetime maid."

"What did you say this is?"

"The bride price. I have been bargaining with the family."

"I don't understand what you mean, Ah Mah."

"I have matched you with a nice, rich family. Your fiancé is a very kind young man. We had chosen a wedding date in the summer, after you would be out of school. But they are afraid that your future father-in-law cannot live until then. He is very ill. That's why they have changed the date to today. We have known the family for quite a long time, though this is still very rushed, I admit."

"Do you mean I'm going to *get married*?"

"Please don't raise your voice to me!"

"Oh . . . I'm sorry . . . I didn't mean to."

Ah Choi returned with a heavily embroidered red-and-gold wedding gown and headpiece, and carefully hung them on a clothing stand. Then she left. Seeing those, I knew Ah Mah was serious.

"I'm too young, Ah Mah! I never thought that I would be getting married *this* soon. Ah Mah, *please, please* let me go home." I was about to cry.

"This *is* your home, and I'm your father's mother, Ying. I have the right to do what I think is best for you."

"But I'm only eleven, Ah Mah."

"I know that. When I married your grandfather, I was not much older than you. So, I have made an agreement with the family, the same kind of agreement my father had with your great-grandfather. You'll share a bed with your mother-in-law until you reach eighteen. Then you'll begin to share a bedroom with your husband."

"But that was a long time ago, Ah Mah. It is 1948 now!"

"Don't argue with me! Ah Choi will help you get ready. They will come to get you at nine."

"No, please don't, Ah Mah. Please let me go home," I begged her.

"It's no use crying. All your dowry furniture has already been delivered to the bride's room. Everything is finalized." She hobbled off, pretending not to hear me.

It made me so mad. I followed Ah Mah and said, "I am *not* going to get married!"

"Young lady! How dare you disobey me! When your grandfather told me I was getting married, even though I didn't like it, I dared not say no to my father! How dare you talk to me like that! What has your Ah Pau been teaching you?" Her sharp eyes stared straight into mine as if she were going to mesmerize me into submission.

"Do not compare me with you! I am going home!" I rushed back to my room, changed into my own clothes, pulled the coils out of my hair, and started to leave. But the front door was now secured with a rusty chain and metal lock. It dawned on me that Ah Mah had sent Ah Choi to lock the door while I was in the room.

I should have tried to leave immediately instead of going to my room. I felt angry and upset. Ah Mah was making decisions for me and giving me no right to disagree, no right to question her, no right to my own say. I went back to my room, threw myself on the bed, and wept bitterly.

Chapter 8

I was really scared. How I wished Ah Pau or Kee, Auntie or Ah So were here! Oh, Ah So! Last year, my cousin Ah So had escaped from becoming a concubine to a man named Ghost Walk. Yes! I would escape like she did! It was my only chance! I couldn't just lie there on the bed and feel sorry for myself. I had to escape before nine o'clock. Ah Mah had said the groom's family would be coming to get me then.

I inspected the room. There was no other window except the small one located high in the corner.

There was a wardrobe beneath the window. . . . But how could I reach the top? The wardrobe was taller than I was. I looked around and saw the bench. I closed the door so they wouldn't know what I was doing. I didn't hear much commotion in the living room—only the old clock making a *tick-tock* sound. I moved the bench in front of the wardrobe. But I still couldn't reach the top!

I got down and tried to move the chest of drawers, but it wouldn't budge. I thought about the drawers. There were two small ones and four big ones. All of them were empty, except for the one that held my new clothes and shoes. I took them out and stacked the drawers crisscrossed on the bench, with the small ones on top. The stack of drawers wobbled when I climbed up to the top of the wardrobe. Fortunately, the wardrobe was steady. I tried to stand up. It was scary. I could tell my legs were trembling until I took hold of the iron bars on the window. They were solid! As I was trying to figure out how to get past the bars, I heard someone knock on the front door of the house. The knocking was rapid and loud and sounded like an emergency.

What does it mean? I wondered. Panicking, I almost fell off the wardrobe. Perhaps in a few minutes I would hear the trumpets and flutes, signaling the arrival of the bride's sedan chair. I could almost imagine being grabbed and carried off to the groom's house.

I desperately tried to shake the bars with all my might. I told myself it was my *only* chance. But it was no use. I had to think of another way. Maybe I could squeeze my body between the bars.

I hoisted myself up on the windowsill. I could just barely squeeze my head through the bars. Great! But when I looked outside, my heart jumped. Instead of the roof of another house, there was only an empty lot next door. There was no way I could jump down from a twelve-foot-high wall, even if I could get myself out the window. I needed a rope or something. So I tried to pull my head back. *Oh, no!* I was stuck! I twisted around, but it didn't help.

While I was struggling, my neck got sore from being in such an awkward position. Then I heard the door open.

"Help me!" I yelled.

"Aiyah!" was all I heard from Ah Choi.

Ah Mah uttered a sharp cry and Ah Choi began saying, "Mrs. Yeung, Mrs. Yeung!" I couldn't see them, but I figured Ah Mah must have fainted when she saw me.

The strong scent of Tiger Balm ointment suffused the room. Ah Choi must have been massaging it into Ah Mah's temples to revive her.

I don't know how long I stayed in that awkward position. Finally, a man used a long bamboo ladder to climb up to the window from outside and sawed one of the iron bars in half so I could get my head out.

I felt as if my neck would never be straight again, but I didn't care. I was already figuring that since the bar was broken, I still had a chance to escape. But the man didn't leave. He immediately began to replace the broken bar from outside. Ah Mah and Ah Choi had returned to the living room when I came down. Now I realized that I didn't remember hearing trumpets and flutes. Was it nine o'clock yet? I didn't know. Anyway, I had to tell Ah Mah that I *must* be going, even though I didn't know how to get back to the ferry.

Ah Mah was lying on one of the recliners with her eyes closed. There was a letter on her lap. Ah Choi was standing faithfully beside her, but Auntie Three was nowhere in sight.

I sensed that something had happened. I looked at the old clock on the wall. It was already fifteen minutes after ten. I didn't want to find out what was going on. I needed to tell Ah Mah that I must leave. But she only opened her eyes with great difficulty, and then said, "The Lo family has postponed the wedding until tomorrow. Something has happened. You belong here. You must stay."

"I'm sorry, Ah Mah. I must go back to Ah Pau. She isn't well," I told her, trying my best not to raise my voice. Ah Mah closed her eyes again and didn't appear to be upset by what I said. I stood there for a second and said, "Ah Mah, take care."

She ignored me, so I followed Ah Choi to the kitchen and asked her for the key. She began making a fire with pine straw, and the whole kitchen was filled with smoke. She motioned me to ask Ah Mah. I knew what the result would be, so I headed straight for the back courtyard door. It was locked, just like the front door. I kicked the door hard, and almost broke my toes. As I was moaning from the pain and my helplessness, Auntie Three, who had already changed into a regular *tong cheong sam*, came out of the outhouse.

"What's wrong?" she asked.

Tears streamed down my cheeks. "Auntie Three, please help me," I sobbed.

At once, she motioned me to be quiet. I understood. I felt better. At least someone would stand by my side in this house.

I lowered my voice and said, "I don't want to get married."

"I heard the news," she whispered. "But why not? You are very lucky. You wouldn't have to worry about being hungry for the rest of your life. . . . If I had a daughter, I would encourage her to grab that chance."

"You don't understand. Ah Pau is sick, and she needs me." I felt almost as though Auntie Three were my mother, so I could be frank with her.

"Oh, I see."

We heard Ah Choi's footsteps approaching the well in the back courtyard. Auntie raised her voice on purpose and said, "Let's go back to the house. It looks like it's going to rain soon."

Chapter 9

I was hungry, but I didn't eat lunch. I wanted to show Ah Mah how strongly I resented her arranging the marriage. She and Ah Choi didn't seem to care if I ate or not. But they did care what I was doing. Ah Choi kept her eyes on me all day long. I was planning not to eat supper, either. Then I had second thoughts. I needed energy for my escape.

As we started supper, Ah Mah seized the opportunity to lecture me: "Act like a young lady from a wealthy family. I don't want to lose face in front of other people."

"Yes, Ah Mah," I whispered, concealing my anger so she wouldn't suspect me.

"After tomorrow, you'll belong to the Lo family. I want you to watch your behavior and act responsibly. I don't want you to ruin their reputation or become the subject of gossip."

With a disgusted look on her face, Auntie Three stood up abruptly and walked away from the table. I didn't know what was going on between the two of them.

"You can eat now. But mind your manners."

"Yes, Ah Mah."

I ate like a pig, and afterward I felt stuffed. When I stepped into the back courtyard to go to the outhouse, Auntie Three was standing next to the back courtyard door, whispering to a man outside. The man dashed away, but I already recognized him as the sedan-chair bearer with the nasty scar over his eyebrow.

Auntie Three quickly closed the door and put the lock and chain back on the wooden latch. It dawned on me that I could have just dashed out while she was talking to the man. But it was too late now. I had missed the chance. She was holding the key and a small brown paper bag. She smiled at me uneasily. "Oh, Little Princess. Ah Fu just got me some *seh yeuk*. Ah Fu is our day laborer. He lives in the back alley. But Ah Mah doesn't like me to ask Ah Fu to run errands. She doesn't like me going out to play mah-jongg, either. You know, I can't be like her, always praying or reading. I need to go out. I need something to do to pass the time."

Perhaps that was why she and Ah Mah didn't get along, I thought. But I felt even closer to Auntie Three because she shared her frustrations over Ah Mah with me. I wanted to ask her for the key, but I heard Ah Choi calling to the cat, which was eating and didn't pay any attention to

63

Ah Choi. Auntie Three walked to the cat dish. She kicked the cat away. The cat let out a sharp cry and dashed off. There was less than half a bowl of rice. She poured some of the *seh yeuk* powder into the bowl and began to mix it with the rice. I wanted to ask her if the powder would hurt the cat. I thought about my own cat back in Tai Kong. I also began to worry about the boy who would probably eat the cat food, but I couldn't worry about anyone else right now. The most urgent thing was to get out of this prison house as soon as possible.

Ah Choi picked up the cat and retreated to the house.

"Auntie Three," I said, peering toward the kitchen to make sure that Ah Choi was not there. Then I squatted down, watching as she continued to mix the powder into the rice. "Auntie Three, please help me."

"Oh, Little Princess! You know I want to help you; I can't stand the way they treat you. But I can't say anything, you know. Your Ah Mah is the boss."

"I know, but you are the only one who can help me, Auntie Three."

"How?"

"Please open the back courtyard door and let me leave."

"You're not joking, are you?"

"No, I'm not. Perhaps you can just tell me where they keep the key."

"I'll get into trouble if I tell you, Little Princess."

"Please, Auntie Three. I need to go back home."

"Well . . . when do you plan to go this time?"

"I need to get out of this house before tomorrow

morning. So, I'm planning to leave tonight, after everybody has gone to bed."

Her eyes looked strange suddenly. "Okay. But you have to promise not to tell *anybody* that I told you."

"Even if I get caught, I will *never* betray you, Auntie Three," I said sincerely.

"It's usually kept behind the kitchen door, but I cannot guarantee it will be there later."

"I know," I said.

Ah Choi came out, carrying a washpan to the gutter next to the outhouse. But I noticed that her eyes were on the cat dish. I got up and walked toward the bathhouse.

Right after I washed, the sky clouded and suddenly turned dark, like india ink. That upset me. I was nervous, but tried my best not to show any sign. I wanted to let Ah Mah think that I was an obedient grandchild, willing to do whatever she asked. So I stayed in the living room, acting like a rich young lady and watching Ah Choi fold clothes on the daybed. Auntie Three was out again. Ah Mah was reading in the recliner next to a kerosene lamp. I was bored to death and anxious to know if they had put the key where it was supposed to be. To avoid looking suspicious, I waited until nine o'clock.

"I'm ready to go to bed," I finally announced. I took a kerosene lamp with me to the outhouse. Very cautiously, I stole a look at the back of the kitchen door. My heart jumped! The key was there. I had the urge to just get the key and open the door leading out of the back courtyard. But how about all my belongings? I also thought about getting the key first, but then I had second thoughts. Ah Choi might need to open that door for Auntie Three or something. Then my plan would be unmasked. I headed for the outhouse. I was still trembling when I came back. I took several deep breaths to calm myself down before I entered the house. Then I said good night to Ah Mah and went to my bedroom.

I put on my own shoes and packed my old clothes and clogs in the bundle. Ah Choi had fanned the mosquito net for me. I blew out the lamp and sat on the bed, afraid I would fall asleep if I lay down.

Immediately I pictured Ah Pau, looking dull-eyed, lying on the daybed with food next to her, untouched. She was moaning from back pain, and I was not there for her. No one was there for her. My eyes started to moisten and my nose started running. I was afraid to cry, afraid that someone would hear me. So I covered my mouth and closed my eyes, imagining Ah Pau standing in front of me in the dark. *Ah Pau, I will be with you soon. Ah Pau, I won't let you be all by yourself. Ah Pau, you must have known what Ah Mah was going to ask of me. You must have known, because you told me you had to obey, even though you didn't agree. . . . I know you must have had a lot of pressure from Ah Mah, and I won't be mad at you. I will take good care of you because you have always taken care of me. I will get the key, then I will leave this rotten house, even though I don't know how to get home. But I will be okay. Everything will be okay as long as I leave this house.*

Boom! I was awakened by thunder that sounded like it was right over the roof. I had been asleep! I panicked. I hoped it was not yet dawn, because Ah Choi got up very early. If she was already up, I would have lost my last chance to escape!

I picked up my belongings and tiptoed cautiously out of my room. The living room was dark and quiet, except for the flickering of the kerosene lamp and the sound of rain hitting the roof. Dawn had not yet arrived. Despite the rain, I sneaked out. I tiptoed to the kitchen door and searched for the key. I could hardly breathe until I found it. Then I ran toward the back courtyard.

My hand was shaking as I tried to put the key in the lock, as if I were trying to open someone's safe. I couldn't see the keyhole because of the dark and the rain. Lightning struck and brightened up the whole yard, but it came and went like a snake of fire, so quickly that I was still not able to see where to insert the key. I was frustrated. I shook the chain. I heard a dog, growling and barking outside. I was terrified. It would wake up Ah Mah and Ah Choi. Ah Choi would come out to investigate. Sure enough, I heard a commotion in the kitchen. I ran to the storage room where the door was wide open, perhaps blown by the wind. As I slipped in, I almost stepped on a bowl, which started to wobble and make a racket. Then a voice came from deep inside the dark room: "Who are *you*?"

Chapter 10

Oh, no! Ah Mah must have sent people to stop me. And there was no way to get out of here. . . .

A flash of lightning lit up half the storage room through a window. I could tell that about two-thirds of the room was full of pine straw, stacked high. But I didn't know where the voice came from, until I heard it again from the top of the stacked pine straw. "Who *are* you?"

"Shush!" I dashed behind the door when I saw a light. I peered out through the crack between the door and the wall. Someone wearing a pointed bamboo hat and holding a kerosene lamp was checking the lock on the back courtyard door, the one I had tried to open. It looked like Ah Choi. Then the light moved closer, and I could hear the sound of her clogs and the sound of raindrops on her bamboo hat. Ah Choi was coming into the storage room! I would be a goner for sure. I tried to hold my breath but I still could hear my heart thumping. There was no way out. I stood still, closed my eyes, and waited for Ah Choi's kerosene lamp to expose me completely. Just at that moment, I heard the door hinge creak, the sound of the storage room door closing, and the latch being fastened.

"*Aiyah*," I exclaimed under my breath. I was relieved, yet worried at the same time. How could I get out of the storage room?

"I can just use a finger to open that old latch," the voice came again, this time quietly. I was sure it was a boy's voice. But it was not threatening.

I looked up. I could see two eyes shining brilliantly in the dark. I had the feeling that he had not been sent by Ah Mah, but perhaps was the one who stole the cat's food. I didn't have time to ask him about that. I whispered, not taking any chances, in a shaky voice, "I need help. I need to get out of this house."

"You don't have to worry about that lady," he whispered back.

How could he be so sure? But I didn't have time to discuss it with him. I said, "Would you help me if I give you ten *yuan*?"

"Ten *yuan*!" The boy jumped down from the pine straw and demanded, "Where is it? Give it to me first."

Lightning again illuminated the storage room. I could see a small face with a pair of big, sparkling eyes, almost covered up by stringy hair.

I took the money out of my pocket. It was still dry. It was a big sum of money, but money was not a priority to me then. Time was. Ah Pau was.

I held the money in front of me, close to my body, and said, "How do we get out? A dog is outside and the door is—"

I thought about the key.

"The dog only barks. It doesn't bite."

"I lost the key! I don't know where the key is! Maybe I dropped it a while ago."

"We don't need the key to the back courtyard door."

"But how we are going to get out?"

"Just trust me."

I gave the bill to him doubtfully and said, "I have to hurry."

The boy just used one finger to push up the latch, and the storage door opened. It made a creaking sound. We peered at the kitchen. It was dark. Ah Choi must have gone back to sleep. The boy ordered, "Go to the big tree!"

"Why?"

"You don't trust me, do you?"

"I do," I said. I didn't have a choice, so I quickly went out with him.

The rain soaked both of us, and I felt chilled immediately. As the boy got ready to climb the tree I warned, "No, we'll be struck by lightning."

"Who says?"

"Everybody knows that," I told him. But he didn't listen to me. He climbed up into the big banyan tree like a monkey.

"Hurry, before the lightning comes again!" He reached down to help me. The dog started to growl again. The boy kept saying, "Easy, easy," and the dog settled down.

I hesitated, frightened about getting struck by lightning. Yet I was also worried that Ah Choi could come out to the back courtyard again.

I handed him my basket and the bundle of clothes and climbed up the big trunk, edging onto the branch that extended over the wall.

"Jump!" he called through the heavy rain after he was on the ground. *I need to jump before the lightning strikes,* I thought. So I closed my eyes and leaped. At that very instant, lightning flashed. The whole alley was lit up like daylight, and I was glad I had already left the tree.

The dog saw me and barked. It barked so loudly that I was sure everyone living on the alley would be awakened soon.

"Walk fast, but don't run," the boy instructed me while he tried to soothe the dog.

My heart tightened when I heard a door open. I looked back. A shadow that looked like Ah Fu was moving in front of another house. He was coming after us! Just as we got out of the alley into another narrow street, the boy commanded, "Over there!"

We started to run. I turned to the left. I couldn't see much in front of me because it was raining so hard. I just obeyed the boy's orders, not having any idea what we would run into. We turned several times and ended up in an alley with no exit. I panicked. I was sure that I would be captured when Ah Fu caught up. But the boy said,

"Come here!" I started to follow him to a house just next to us.

Then I stood frozen. One round white lantern hung at each side of the door on the porch. The candles inside the lanterns had already burned out, but it wasn't hard to tell that they were funeral lanterns—the symbol of a death in the family.

"I don't want to go into this house," I said firmly.

"Why not? It's the only way to get away from him."

He was right. Who would want to go into someone's house while they had a dead body there? I didn't have any choice. It was either go in, or get caught.

The wailing sound in the house was weak, about to die down, even though the house was full of people. Exhausted, the mourners were all kneeling, except for the children, who had already fallen asleep on the floor. The men and children had white headbands wrapped around their foreheads, while the women had white cloths wrapped into pointed hats and covering their faces.

The house was lit up by white candles. The dead body lay on the bed in the corner and was covered with a white cloth, except for the head. A table next to the body was full of untouched dishes of food, bowls of rice, and chopsticks. Candles burned weakly at each corner of the table. Nobody was eating. The meal was for the dead person and his new friends in the next world. Everybody was tired, even the *see kung*, who was wearing a big gold robe and a black square hat. He was supposed to spread out his arms and hit a small drum to chase the ghosts away, but he appeared to be dozing in the old chair next to the table.

I followed the boy, slipping toward the corner away from the door where he picked up a couple of white funeral garments. He handed one to me and said, "Put this on and kneel down like them, so the family will not recognize us."

"*Dai gut lai see!* I didn't have a death in my family!" I spat on the floor to rid myself of the jinx and refused to take the funeral hood.

He tied the white headband around his forehead. "Hurry up!" he whispered. "Ah Fu will be looking for us!"

I felt the white material descend over my head suddenly, and the boy at once let out a loud wail, full of energy. I followed suit, wailing from my lungs, as if I were one of the mourners.

I don't know how long we wailed until I suddenly realized that I was the only person crying. I peered over to where the boy had been. He was gone! Just as I began to fear that I had been left behind, someone cried, "The wild child! The wild child!"

I could hardly believe my eyes! The boy was sitting on one of the benches, eating. How could he do that? The food was for the dead! And the *see kung* was staring at the boy, with his eyes and mouth wide open, as though he were seeing a ghost, until someone shouted, "Catch him! Catch the wild child!"

I pulled off the white funeral hood and sprang up, grabbing my belongings and calling to him, "Go! Go! They're going to catch you!"

A man was about to grab the boy from behind. At first, the boy looked startled, but then he deftly sprang to his feet and jumped up onto the table, stepping all over the dishes of food. "Catch him! Catch him!" The whole house was in disorder except for the corpse.

The *see kung* stretched his wide sleeves out, hoping to snare the boy, but he dashed aside, avoiding the man's grasp. Two men surrounded the table to pin the boy down but he was jumping around on the table, trying to avoid being caught.

Suddenly the *see kung* screamed, "Fire! Fire!" At first, I was confused, until I saw the *see kung* dancing a jig in panic. There was smoke rising from his wide, floppy sleeves.

The funeral party seemed numb, until someone commanded, "Water! Get water!"

"Drop and roll!" the boy, who was still standing on top of the table, yelled at the *see kung*. But the *see kung* was jumping with fear. The boy leaned over to the edge of the table and pushed the *see kung*, yelling, "Drop to the floor!"

The *see kung* fell down, screaming, "Fire!"

"Roll! Roll!" the boy ordered, but the *see kung* was too panicked and just lay still, howling and moaning. Fortunately, several men had already gotten buckets of water, which they poured on him, drenching the *see kung* and putting out the fire at the same time.

The *see kung* lay still, sputtering water from his nose and mouth. Suddenly, he sprang up and roared, "You! You!" As he was just about to choke the boy, someone discovered me.

"That girl, too! That girl, too!"

Before I could react, someone grabbed me. I strug-

74

gled, trying to save the boy, yelling, "Stop it! Stop it! You're going to strangle him!" But the *see kung* didn't give up. Just as the boy seemed to be about to pass out, I screamed, "A pregnant cat! Someone let in a pregnant cat!"

The whole house was filled with horror, including the person who was holding me.

"Where? Where?"

"There!" the grip on my arms loosened. I pointed to a dark corner, "There! It's going toward the dead body!"

"No!" The *see kung* released his grip on the boy's neck and commanded, "Catch the cat! Don't let it cross the body! Oh, my!" he cried, closing both eyes and chanting something.

While all the people were searching nervously for the cat, I grabbed the boy and yelled, "Run!" I didn't think of anything else at that moment—not Ah Fu, not Ah Mah. I only thought of getting away from the house before they discovered I was playing a trick.

"Are you all right?" I asked when we stopped to rest.

"Yes," he said, coughing and massaging his throat. "Thank you for saving my life."

"Don't mention it. Hurry before they come out to get us."

It was almost dawn. The rain had stopped. I had a better look. We were on a narrow, winding street with dilapidated brick houses. The air was much fresher outside, and nobody was in sight. While we walked quickly away from the dead end, I feared Ah Fu was hiding somewhere. "How do we get out of the town? I want to hurry."

We stopped at an abandoned house. The boy said, "We'll take a shortcut. Get inside before anybody spots us."

It was quite dark inside. We groped our way to a trap-door in the kitchen. Underneath the trapdoor was a hole barely large enough for one person to squeeze through. He told me to get in.

"Where does it lead?"

"Outside the town."

It was pitch-dark. A strong, musty odor rushed into my nostrils. I let him go first.

We shuffled along.

"Why did the *see kung* yell not to let the cat cross the body?" the boy asked.

"A dead body will rise up if it is crossed by a pregnant cat."

"Why?"

"I don't know. Everybody says that."

"No wonder they were so scared."

After a while, we made our way out of the tunnel. I could see a faint outline of a small hill against the dawning sky.

"Is this the outskirts of the town?"

"Yes. We'll go to my house first."

"I can't stay. I have to go back to Tai Kong. I have to get to the ferry," I said, although I was tired and very sleepy. Still, I was glad that I was already out of Ah Mah's prison house.

"I haven't seen you in that house before. Why do you have to run away? Are they going to sell you somewhere?"

I told him about the wedding.

He laughed.

"It's not funny," I said.

"I'm sorry," he said. "In that case, we can't stay here for long. I am afraid they will come here since they know you are with me."

"Do people know you live here?"

"Some people know. But they never come and bother me."

"Well, I don't want to go to your house."

"I think it'll be okay to stay there just a little while. Besides that, we cannot leave for the ferry until the sky is completely bright. Otherwise, people will shoot if you go into their territory."

"Who? The bandits?"

"Yes, they have their own territories."

I shivered.

I knew I should listen to his advice, since he knew this area well.

There was no path leading to the hill, and the weeds were knee-deep. I was scared I would step on a snake. It was not light enough to see what was on the ground. But snakes didn't seem to bother the boy. He walked as though he were on a street. I tried to follow where he had stepped, hoping not to encounter any slithery creatures.

When we were just about halfway to the hill, I could see that the whole place was full of graves. Some rotten coffins were sticking halfway out of the ground. Broken golden pots revealed grayish bones, which relatives had dutifully dug up from their loved one's graves and placed in the funerary pots to be preserved. I shivered all over. I feared I would step on those bones, and then I would be in big trouble.

We reached the middle of the hill. A small, deserted, deteriorating temple stood among some thick bushes. I thought his house must be around there, but he suddenly said, pointing to the deserted temple, "That's my house."

"What?"

Chapter 11

One wall of the red brick temple was torn down. The light inside the temple was dim, but a strong odor of incense and candles rushed into my nostrils. Various sizes of brass burners on the worship table were still full of incense and candles. Spiderwebs draped worship statues of the thunder god, earth god, and river god.

"You can rest on my bed," he said, pointing to the space underneath the worship table. A piece of ragged, dirty cloth was spread on the floor, with a pillow made of a bundle of rolled-up rags. There was no way I would sleep there. It was probably full of lice and bedbugs. I had already noticed that the boy kept scratching himself.

"No, I'll just squat down and close my eyes for a few seconds."

I was exhausted and felt chilled, and I sneezed several times in a row. I needed to change into dry clothes, but I just wanted to close my eyes.

Probably sensing my unwillingness to sleep in his bed, the boy said, "I'm going to get some weeds." He went out. Not long afterward, he returned holding a big bundle of weeds. He spread the weeds next to the place where I was squatting and said, "I'm going to make you a new bed."

"Oh, thanks," I said, relieved. Even though they were damp, the sweet, fresh smell of the weeds was much more pleasant than the incense smell of the temple. The early morning light shone through the missing temple wall and fell on the boy's stringy, tangled hair. I noticed that his hair was not black, but brown! It reminded me of the boy who had run away when we were arriving at Ah Mah's house. Was it him? I was sure he must be the one who ate the cat's food. Now I was completely awake.

I asked him if he had eaten the cat's food with the *seh yeuk*.

"What if I did?"

"Did you get sick?"

"Do I look sick?"

It was strange. I saw Auntie Three pour the *seh yeuk* into the rice. When I was talking to him, I looked squarely into his gaunt, filthy face. His big eyes were brown, but not as dark as mine, and his eyelashes were thick and curly, unlike my straight eyelashes. I exclaimed, "You look funny!" I was immediately curious. Who were his parents? He looked like he had mixed blood.

He ignored my statement and returned the ten-*yuan* bill to me, saying, "I don't want your money. I want to make a deal with you."

"What kind of deal?" I asked, looking straight into his funny-colored eyes, which showed a sparkle of brightness and vitality as they gleamed.

"I want to go with you. I know this area very well. I know how to get around without being seen by the bandits because I know their territories. You need my help, and I will do anything you say if you'll let me go with you."

"You mean all the way to Tai Kong?"

"Yes. I like you. You saved my life and—and you treat me like your friend. You don't yell at me like others do."

I felt flattered. "What's your name? My name is Ying—Yeung Ying."

"My name is..." he hesitated, then said timidly, "On On."

"On On?" I asked. "How do you write it?"

"I don't know," he murmured. "People call me Wild Child when they chase me away."

"Oh, I'm sorry. Do you know how old you are?"

He shook his head and said, "I know you are going to laugh at me again."

"No. I won't. Let me see." Using my hand as a measurement, I compared his height to mine. "I am eleven. You are shorter than me, so you must be nine or ten."

"I don't know."

"Where are your parents?"

He didn't answer me. His thick eyelashes lowered like two fans. Then he said, "I don't know where my parents are. I have never seen them."

I felt very heavy inside. "But who raised you?"

"My Ah Pau."

"Oh, my Ah Pau is raising me, too." Suddenly, I felt close to him. "My parents moved to Hong Kong when I was five. Since then I've lived with my Ah Pau and my uncle and his family."

"Really? But my Ah Pau was not really my mother's mother. She didn't know who my parents were, either. She found me on the roadside when I was a baby and brought me to her house to live."

"Where is your Ah Pau now?"

"She died."

"Didn't she have any children or relatives you could stay with?"

"She had a daughter, but I have forgotten her name. One day, I overheard her husband saying he was going to sell me to someone because they couldn't afford to keep me. So I ran away."

I thought about Uncle, Auntie, Kee, and Ah So. I knew that they would not sell me if Ah Pau passed away. I felt that I was far luckier than the boy.

"Do you know where you ran away from?"

"I couldn't find the way back. It was a long time ago. But I can take care of myself."

"Do you always sleep in someone's storage room?"

"Not really. Only once in a while at your Ah Mah's house. Please don't let your Ah Mah know. Nobody knows, except the old lady."

"Who? Ah Choi?"

"I don't know her name. Not the one who screamed

at me but the one who always does house chores. The first time I stayed in the storage room, I think she discovered me on the pine straw, but she just turned her head and pretended not to see me."

"Why?"

"I don't know. That's why I came back. It's much warmer in the storage room than in the temple. I can cover myself with the thick pine straw."

I said, "You can come with me. You can stay with us." I wasn't thinking about whether he knew the way back to Tai Kong.

"I can? Good! Oh, is there any man in your house?"

"Yes. There's Kee and my uncle. But my uncle is not living with us now."

"Will Kee sell me?"

"No, he won't."

"Oh, good!" He was so thrilled that he smiled. I could see his teeth were stained and dark. He said, "You sleep and I will find some food for us to eat on the way to Tai Kong."

Before I could ask him where he could find food, he was already gone. I couldn't stay awake any longer. I dropped onto the fresh weed bed to just close my eyes for a minute.

Chapter 12

I suddenly awoke from a funny dream. In my dream, someone was screaming, "Run! Run!" It took me a few seconds to realize I was inside the strange, deserted temple. I looked at the bed underneath the worship table. It was empty. I heard footsteps and recalled that the boy had gone to get food. I dropped my head back on the weeds.

With my eyes still closed, I mumbled, "Is that you?"

No answer. I thought I must be dreaming, until I heard a man's voice: "Little Princess . . ."

Ah Fu was right in front of me, with a long rope coiled in his hand. The screaming voice was more audible. It wasn't a dream. At once, I pulled my thoughts together and jumped up. Before I could reach the missing wall to escape, something hit me hard from behind. I felt my chest encircled. I was being dragged backward.

"Did *you* win or did I?" Ah Fu asked and pulled me up roughly.

"Let me go! Let me go!" I tried hard to push the rope up over my head, but I couldn't. He wrapped the rope around me several times, then hoisted me onto his shoulder and began to walk down the hill.

"Let me go!" I screamed, wriggling.

"Shut up!" Ah Fu roared.

I heard hasty footsteps. The boy yelled, "Let her go!"

The boy was holding Ah Fu's leg and wouldn't let go. They were struggling. Ah Fu almost dropped me.

"Get away, you wild child!"

Then I heard a sharp cry and a bump. I knew Ah Fu had kicked the boy.

"Are you all right?" I yelled, kicking my legs with all my might. While Ah Fu continued to walk, I spotted the boy lying on the dirt, struggling to get up, with blood trickling from his nose. Then suddenly he sprang up.

"Don't! He'll hurt you!" I knew what the boy was going to do. I heard a loud kicking sound.

Then all of a sudden, Ah Fu dropped me, and I rolled down the hill a few feet and was stopped by a bush. I heard Ah Fu moan in pain. Before I knew what was happening, the boy ran toward me and shouted, "Hurry! Hurry!"

"I can't . . . I can't . . . " I struggled frantically with the rope. He quickly helped me with it.

Just as I was getting free, the boy warned, "Here he comes! Run!"

I sprang to my feet, not knowing which direction to take. I ran toward an open field dotted with bushes. Suddenly, I heard the boy scream frantically, "Not there! Not there!"

It was too late! I heard something whistling through the air. At once, I fell flat and lay still on the ground, burying my face in the dirt. My heart beat furiously.

I lay prostrate, afraid to move. I heard the boy let out a sharp cry. I dared not raise up my head to look back, because I also heard some footsteps coming closer and closer. I just lay still, wondering what my fate would be. Perhaps they would just shoot me right on the spot. Suddenly a man yelled, "A girl!"

Someone jerked me up. I heard a voice respond far away. I was trembling all over. I couldn't hear the conversation or even stand up. I felt I had borrowed someone else's legs. My mind was blank. All I knew was that I was being dragged away. I didn't know where they were taking me or who they were until I was finally dumped onto a hard floor. It seemed a long time before I could pull myself together and think clearly. But I was still alive.

"You ran into my territory," a man finally spoke. I knew for sure I was going to die or be sold to somebody else. I wished Ah Pau was with me. I needed her to tell me I would be all right, to give me a cup of cold tea and calm me down.

"What's your name?"

I could barely raise my head. My neck felt out of joint. I saw a man with a round face, sitting next to a table. *Perhaps he's a bandit*, I thought.

I tried to swallow, but my mouth was as dry as cotton.

"Yeung Ying." I could hardly speak. I was still trembling.

"What? Speak out loudly."

I repeated myself. Then he asked me a lot of questions. I told him I was not from around there. I had run away from my Ah Mah, who wanted me to get married. I didn't know what street Ah Mah lived on. Then I burst into tears.

"What's your Ah Mah's name?"

"Yeung Yee."

"Yeung Yee! Is that the one whose daughter-in-law loves to play mah-jongg?"

Did he mean Auntie Three? So I replied, "My Ah Mah has bound feet and lives in a big house."

"That's her. I remember her well. She helped my cousin write letters to his son and never asked anything in return. But her daughter-in-law gambles too much and gives your Ah Mah a lot of headaches." He motioned someone to come in and whispered to a rough-looking man. Then he said to me, "You should not run around in this dangerous area."

The man left, then returned minutes later. He grabbed my arm and took me out. Without telling me anything, he quickly tied my hands behind my back. Before I could ask him why he had to do that, he stuffed a foul cloth into my mouth. It almost made me gag. I couldn't yell. Then he picked me up and dumped me inside a large woven basket. Without saying a word, he pushed my head down into the basket and put the lid on.

He must have used a rope to secure the lid, because no matter how hard I tried to raise my head, the basket wouldn't open. Then I felt myself being hoisted up and carried away.

At once, a horrible thought flashed into my mind—he was going to drown me in a pond, the death sentence given to unfaithful women long ago. At this life-and-death moment, I couldn't think of anything except survival. So I tried hard to kick, but my legs were squashed. The man yelled for me to stop wiggling. I didn't listen to him. Instead, I tried to free my hands, which were turning numb from the lack of circulation. I could not loosen the rope even a little. It seemed like a long time passed. Finally, I felt as if I was being thrown from a high place into the water. . . .

Chapter 13

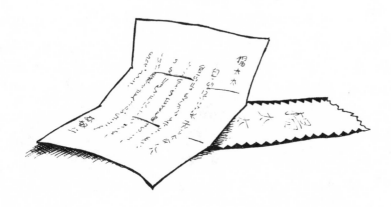

But the basket hit the ground. Weeping and trembling, I heard someone knocking on a door. After a while, I heard the door open. Had he decided to sell me?

I heard the man talking. I tried to yell "Help!" but no words came out. Then I heard Ah Choi calling for Ah Mah. The basket was lifted again and dumped on the ground. Someone removed the lid. It was Ah Choi. She pulled the foul cloth from my mouth and freed my hands while Ah Mah thanked the man and gave him money. I climbed out of the basket and slumped to the ground, weeping. I longed for someone to embrace me, to tell me that I was all right.

I heard Ah Mah let out a sigh. Then she said in a monotone voice, "I don't have any idea how you ended up like this."

"I tried to get away from Ah Fu," I whispered.

But Ah Mah didn't seem to hear me. She continued, "Early this morning, Ah Choi delivered a letter to the Lo family and asked them to postpone the wedding because you ran away. You are as stubborn as a mule. I'm going to write a second letter in order to cancel the marriage. Ah Choi will take it to them as soon as possible. Tomorrow she will accompany you back to your Ah Pau."

Tears trickled down my cheeks. If she had decided that earlier, I wouldn't have gone through all my ordeal. Trying not to shed any more tears, I whispered, "Thank you, Ah Mah." I was still incredulous that I was safe in the house.

"Go clean up and get ready for lunch," was all she said before shuffling back to the living room.

I tried to get up. It took me a while before I could walk.

When I went to the back courtyard to draw water from the well, it was still morning. I had left my bundle of clothes in the deserted temple. I remembered being tied up by Ah Fu, and the boy's voice calling, "Not there! Not there!" and the whizzing sound of the bullets. I shook my head hard, trying to put the memory behind me by washing my face with ice-cold well water. As I was washing, Auntie Three came out from the kitchen. She looked as if she had just returned from somewhere.

"Auntie Three!" All of a sudden, I burst into tears.

"Ying, I heard you were back. Don't cry, Little Princess," she said, patting my shoulder. She seemed to be the only comfort I had.

"I can't help it," I said.

"I'm glad you are okay. But for your own sake," Auntie Three looked at my face and asked, "why didn't you just get married instead of taking the risk of being shot?"

I said, "Ah Mah is canceling the marriage. I don't need to run away anymore."

"What?" She suddenly looked very anxious.

"She told me just a while ago. She is giving Ah Choi a letter to deliver to the Lo family. Tomorrow Ah Choi is taking me back to Tai Kong."

"Really? Oh . . ." she said, and her eyes looked strange. Suddenly she announced, "I have something important to do. I must go." She walked back inside the house. I continued to wash.

When I stepped back into the kitchen, I heard Auntie Three having an angry conversation with Ah Choi. When she saw me, she quickly crumpled up something in her hand and threw it into a pile of firewood behind her.

"Is something wrong?" I asked. Ah Choi was dabbing her eyes with her apron and seemed to be crying.

"No, it's nothing," Auntie Three said. Then she put her arm around my shoulder, pushed me gently away from the kitchen, and said tenderly, "Let's go to your bedroom. You need a real rest."

Chapter 14

I was very tired, but I was also afraid to close my eyes. Every time I did, I heard the boy yelling, "Not there! Not there!" Then there were bullets whistling over my head. I saw myself at the edge of death. I feared someone would squash me into the basket again.

When Ah Choi woke me up, it was before dawn the next day.

After a simple breakfast, I said good-bye to Ah Mah. I wanted to say good-bye to Auntie Three, but Ah Choi said she had left much earlier. I asked her where Auntie Three was. Ah Choi said she didn't have any idea.

I was still wearing the same clothes I'd had on when I ran away. Ah Mah, who had suddenly turned into a nice old lady, gave me twenty *yuan* to get some new clothes.

She also suggested that I take my fancy clothes and shoes with me, since they were mine to keep. Instead of using a kerchief to wrap up my clothes, Ah Mah gave me a small wicker suitcase.

I stepped into the sedan chair, the same one I had come in. I was uneasy and afraid of seeing Ah Fu again. Fortunately, he was not one of the bearers. Even if he was, I didn't need to run away from him anymore.

Ah Choi, who looked like she had a lot of things on her mind, accompanied me on the trip. Like before, she walked beside the sedan chair, trying her best to keep up with us.

I was very anxious to get back to my Ah Pau. I thought about her all the time. I had missed her very much. Even though I had just left a few days earlier, it seemed like a whole year. I also thought about the wild child. I was sorry that I couldn't follow through on my promise to him. Worst of all, I didn't even know if he was okay.

As we turned down several narrow streets, I kept looking on both sides, hoping to spot him. But I didn't. Pretty soon we were out of Lam Cheun and beside the sugarcane field. About half an hour later, we arrived at a dirt crossroad with a pagoda on one side and a small shack on the other that I had missed seeing when I first came. I must have been asleep when we passed them. Several people were resting in the pagoda. Behind it, partly hidden, was something bright red and gold. I turned my eyes to the people, hoping that one of them was the boy. As we approached the pagoda, a lady who looked like Auntie Three came toward us. It really was

Auntie Three! She was holding a big bundle. She said to my sedan chair bearers, "Take a rest."

I was so thrilled that I had the chance to say good-bye to her. She smiled at me and said, "Little Princess. Come and have a cup of tea. You are tired."

I wasn't tired, but I let her help me out of the chair. While she was carefully guiding me toward the little shack, I heard Ah Choi cry from behind us, "What are you doing, Mrs. Three!"

I turned to see Ah Choi running frantically toward us. But a man who looked like Ah Fu stopped her. My heart skipped a beat. I questioned Auntie Three, "Is that Ah Fu? Why is Ah Fu here?"

Auntie Three urged me to enter the shack and said, "Don't pay any attention to Ah Choi." Then Auntie Three came in and closed the door behind her. I immediately sensed there was something wrong. The shack was deserted, with trash strewn all around.

"What *is* this place?"

She smiled. "Today *really* is your big day, Little Princess."

I had never seen her face look so distant.

"But Ah Mah has already canceled the marriage."

"Ah Mah, Ah Mah, that sly old fox!" she said, laughing. "She tricked you, and you didn't even know it!"

"How? How did she trick me this time?"

She didn't answer me for a few seconds, but then she said, "If she didn't trick you, then why did she send us here?"

It was as if she had thrown ice water in my face. This

was the first time I thought about why Ah Mah had let me go so easily. Maybe it *was* just a trick!

"If you are smart, you won't give us any trouble."

I still believed Auntie Three was the only one who could help me. I begged, "Will you help me, Auntie Three, just one more time?"

"I'm afraid not. I've been playing a game with you the whole time, too."

I didn't know what she meant. I felt completely lost.

"Put these on and be quick!" She untied the bundle and showed me the same wedding gown and headpiece as before. Then she left the shack.

Like a wildcat, I stomped on the headpiece, smashing it into the filthy dirt floor. Then I trampled the gown.

The door opened and closed again. Auntie Three stood next to the door, with both arms folded across her chest, glaring at me. "You're really hard to deal with, Little Princess. No wonder that sly old fox Ah Mah had to lie to get you to Lam Cheun!"

"I'm not going to marry anybody, Auntie Three! You don't understand. I need to go back to my Ah Pau. She is sick, and she is alone."

She studied my face for a few seconds, then said calmly, "Do you know what has happened to your Ah Pau?"

"What?" My heart began beating rapidly. I didn't want *anything* to happen to Ah Pau.

"She has been very, very ill since you left. I didn't tell you because I didn't want you to be upset."

"Is she going to die?" I broke into tears.

"Pretty soon, maybe at any minute." Auntie Three

was ready to leave. "It's up to you. If you want to throw a temper tantrum, go ahead. But if you cooperate, *then* you'll see your Ah Pau. It's up to you." She opened the door.

I dashed in front of her and dropped to my knees, despite the dirty floor. Again I begged, "Please, Auntie Three. I'll do *anything* you want me to as long as I can see my Ah Pau."

"Do you mean it?" She closed the door.

"Yes, Auntie Three. I need to take care of my Ah Pau. She is all alone. My uncle probably hasn't gotten my letter yet. Please, I can't let my Ah Pau die. Tell me what you want me to do."

"Okay. First, no screaming, no yelling, no crying, no temper tantrums. Promise?"

"I promise." I wiped my tears, suddenly as meek as a lamb. "Can I go to see my Ah Pau now?"

"No, the wedding will take place in less than an hour. We cannot be late this time. It has been postponed twice already."

"How long will the ceremony last?"

"Not long. You are only a child. We are going to make it as simple as possible. I will help you put on the gown now. Then, all you'll need to do is offer tea to your in-laws and uncles and aunties."

"Can I go home right after that?"

"Sure, Little Princess," Auntie Three promised. "Let's hurry and put on the wedding gown. The groom's family has already sent a sedan chair, and it is right outside."

Now I knew that the bright red-and-gold object I had

seen before was a bride's chair, and it was for me. I picked up the gown. It was soiled and full of wrinkles. I didn't care. All I wanted was to be with my Ah Pau. Auntie Three told me to straighten up the gown. I brushed off as much dirt as I could, then let her help me put it on. It was big, clumsy, heavy, and hot. I didn't complain, though. I would do anything for my Ah Pau.

Auntie Three also helped me rebraid my hair, but she didn't fix it into coils as Ah Choi had done before. She put some rouge on my cheeks. I changed into a pair of embroidered shoes that Auntie Three took from my suitcase. Finally, she helped me put on the bride's headpiece, which was smashed out of shape. I didn't care how I looked. All I wanted to do was get the wedding over with so I could go back to my Ah Pau.

Auntie Three told me to keep my head down, like a shy bride should. As we came out of the shack, I immediately heard the music of trumpets and flutes. I realized it was the musicians who had been resting in the pagoda. Then I heard another voice that sounded like an old lady's: "I'll carry you on my back."

I couldn't see well because my face was covered with a veil made of colorful strings of beads.

Auntie Three leaned close to my ear because of the music. "We've hired her to be your *dai kum*. She will assist you in offering tea. Don't give anybody any trouble."

I said okay. The *dai kum* carried me on her back to the sedan chair. Just as I sat down in the chair, someone closed the door, and the chair was raised up from the ground. I let the bearers carry me wherever they wanted.

All I could think of was Ah Pau, dying in her bed.

It didn't take long to get there. The sedan chair stopped abruptly and the door opened. The *dai kum* came up to the chair and told me to get on her back again.

With the veil in front of my face, I did what the *dai kum* told me. I sensed that she was carrying me into the groom's house because I heard people murmuring that the bride was coming.

Finally, she put me down. I thought we must be in the living room, because it was bright with light and smelled of candles, incense, and oil lamps. The *dai kum* raised her voice and announced enthusiastically, "The bride is here. The bride and groom will offer tea together to his parents!"

I couldn't see who my husband-to-be was, but as the *dai kum* gently pushed me down to kneel on the mat to offer tea, I spotted a skinny, sick-looking old man, dressed in navy blue satin clothes, lying on a recliner, coughing and spitting.

"No! No! I don't want to get married!" I cried out, swinging the *dai kum's* hand away. I heard the clinking sound of china shattering on the clay floor. I pulled off the headpiece and started to run. The room was full of people—men dressed in fancy *tong cheong sams* and women in wedding ceremony dresses, black-and-gold tops with red-and-gold skirts. My sudden action threw the people into panic and confusion. Some women cried out; others murmured and asked Kwun Yum, the goddess of mercy, to bless the ceremony. As I was squeezing through the crowd to find an exit, a couple of men tried to grab me, but I got away, crying again, "No! No! I don't want to get married!"

Then a man grabbed me from behind. I struggled to get loose, but failed. A lady cried, "Don't hurt her! Don't hurt her!"

Another man, the only one with a hat on, warned, "Be gentle with her!"

Something about their faces and voices seemed vaguely familiar, but I didn't have time to look, because someone else shouted, "How disobedient she is! Take her to the bride's room!"

Then the man who had grabbled me from behind picked me up in the air and carried me away, ignoring the cries.

I kicked violently in the air and tried to loosen the man's grip, but he was holding me like a boa constrictor. A couple of ladies cried and guided the man, "Here, here."

Then someone opened the door, and his arms loosened and dropped me. *"Aiyah!"* I let out a cry. I hit the floor hard. One of the ladies tried to help me get up, but the man who dropped me told the ladies to leave. Then someone slammed the door. I tried to stand up, but my back hurt. I lay there quietly for a while, not sure what would happen next.

Finally, I sat up and looked at the room. There was a brand-new bed with a bright red satin coverlet, neatly folded, and a snow-white mosquito net, tied back. A new wardrobe, chest of drawers, and a couple of chairs with a tea table between them—all made out of *seen ji*—were arranged in the room. This must be the dowry furniture that Ah Mah told me had already been delivered to the bride's room! It really was a bride's room. I let out a cry. Now, I had really messed up the whole deal with Auntie Three! Why did I do it? I didn't know. I was angry with myself.

I heard a door creak open on the side of the room next to the bed. I was alert. Again, I tried to get up, but the pain in my back hadn't subsided.

"I am sorry about the way they have been treating you."

Who was it?

Chapter 15

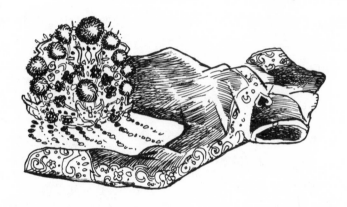

"**I** am not going to hurt you," the man said, coming into the room.

Who was that man? I glanced at his face. He had a tall, straight nose. I had seen that face before, but I couldn't remember where. He was dressed in a very fine quality navy blue satin *tong cheong sam*, just like the old man's. *Ah Mah must have sent him here to keep an eye on me,* I thought.

"I'm going to help you," the man said.

But I couldn't believe him. I couldn't trust anybody around here. Ah Mah had told me that she was going to cancel the marriage, but she was really a fox, as Auntie Three had said. Auntie Three was supposed to be helping me, but she was really on Ah Mah's side. Nobody around here could be trusted, I felt sure, including him.

I kept silent, but was alert in case he came closer to me.

He sat in a chair against the wall, with his back straight and his hands resting on his thighs. He said, "You may not recognize me, but I remember you."

I looked at him, but I still didn't recall who he was.

"I'm Lo Sing. Do you remember that day my schoolmate Wong Chi and I helped you get the kite from the tree?"

"Oh!" I let out a cry. But I still didn't want to ask him why he was here.

"It's past lunchtime now. I know you must be hungry," he said.

I was *very* hungry, but I didn't want to eat. "I want to go back to Tai Kong," I said.

"I'll help you go back."

I looked at him. Should I trust him?

He seemed to read my mind and added, "I know you don't trust me. I don't blame you. My parents tried to arrange our marriage, but we are not yet bride and groom."

"I know. The old man is."

"You mean the one who was lying on the recliner?"

"Yes."

"No. He's my father. I'm supposed to be your husband. I was the one wearing the groom's hat."

"Oh." Now I realized that he was the one who had said, "Be gentle." I had completely forgotten that at a wedding ceremony, the groom always wore a groom's hat while the bride wore a headpiece. I had messed up. And I was confused. "What do you mean 'supposed'? You were not sent by my Ah Mah?"

"No. If you'll give me a chance, I will explain it to you."

I didn't say a word. But I began to believe that he wouldn't do me any harm.

"Do you remember one day two ladies talked to you?"

"When?"

"About two or three weeks ago. I believe they talked with you in Chan Village."

"Oh, you mean Mrs. Tong and her sister."

"Yes, Mrs. Tong is my aunt, my mother's older sister. She wrote to my mother when she accidentally found you."

"What did you mean—accidentally found me?"

"She discovered your lucky red mole."

"Oh, I remember now."

It was on a Sunday morning about a month ago. I had helped Ah Pau carry her worship basket to the temple at the middle of Ford Hill, behind Chan Village. I sat on the granite threshold of the temple doorway to wait for Ah Pau. It was raining. The whole flight of one hundred steps was completely drenched. I feared Ah Pau would fall down and hurt herself. Not long after I sat down, Mrs. Tong, the wife of the owner of the biggest grocery in Tai Kong, sat next to me. She seemed to be waiting for the rain to stop or waiting for her maid to bring her an umbrella. I didn't greet her because I didn't know her personally. I just folded my arms around my knees and gazed at the rain and the mist above the town.

Then I sneezed a couple of times. Mrs. Tong asked

me if I was cold. I told her I just felt a little chilled. Then she leaned over close to me and asked if the tiny red mole on the right side of my upper lip was a mosquito bite or a mole. I told her it was a real mole that had been there as long as I could remember. She then told me it was a rare and precious mole that would make my husband prosper and bring good luck to my children. I didn't take her comment seriously because I hadn't ever thought about getting married and having children. But Mrs. Tong seemed to be inspecting me and told me my looks were very pleasing. Then she asked me how old I was and where I lived. When I told her I lived with Ah Pau in Chan Village, she broke into a big grin and said, "You are the granddaughter of Yeung Yee who lives in Lam Cheun, aren't you?"

I told her I was but I didn't know much about my father's mother. All I remembered was that she walked funny and that she lived in a big house. I didn't think I had been there since I came to live with my Ah Pau. There were bandits along the road. Mrs. Tong told me she didn't know my Ah Mah personally, but her sister lived around that area. Her sister's father-in-law and my grandfather had been very good friends, so both families had known each other for some time. She also told me that my Ah Mah was the only educated woman in that area, a woman of much prestige.

Then Mrs. Tong's maid came, bringing an umbrella, and they left.

I asked Lo Sing, "That means Mrs. Tong's sister is your mother?"

"Yes. She was the one who told my uncle not to hurt you."

"Oh, I heard her. But I didn't quite recognize her voice. Did she come that time just to see my red mole?"

"Yes. She had been searching for a daughter-in-law for a long time without letting me know."

No wonder Ah Pau's face turned pale that day when I told Ah Pau about Mrs. Tong and the lady's visit. I was frightened by Ah Pau's actions. But she hadn't told me what was really bothering her.

"My mother wanted me to accompany her to Tai Kong, but she didn't tell me the purpose of the trip. Now I know why she was so anxious to go to Tai Kong. My mother is very fond of you. She claims that it was the will of heaven for her to find you. She hurried back and sent a matchmaker to your Ah Mah to propose this marriage."

"But I am only eleven."

"She knew that. My father is very ill. He will be gone soon. My mother refuses to accept that fact. She thought that if I got married, the 'double happiness' associated with marriage would stimulate him and would make him well. That's why she has been looking for a wife for me without letting me know.

"At first, your Ah Mah didn't agree because you are still young. Then she changed her mind on the condition that you and my mother share a bed until you reach eighteen. My mother has agreed to whatever your Ah Mah asked for because she wanted the wedding to be held as soon as possible. They had set the date for summer, after school is out. But my father's condition got worse. Mother realized that Father might not live that long, so she changed the wedding date to a few days ago. It was very rushed, but Mother hoped that at least Father could drink the tea offered by his daughter-in-law. That way, I would have my own family before he is gone. You know it is very important to the parents-in-law to be able to drink the tea offered by their daughter-in-law—especially because my father is about to die."

I remembered Ah Mah had said that the groom's father couldn't wait. I remembered she said that it was rushed, but she didn't tell me all the details.

"I didn't know all of that because I was still in Canton going to college. Mother sent someone to bring me home immediately. I thought my father had died. When I found out the truth, I was very angry with my mother and I refused to go along with the wedding, so I hid on the day we were supposed to get married."

Was that the reason someone had knocked on the front door so rapidly that day? Perhaps to inform Ah Mah that the groom had been hiding?

"Then they found me. Mother cried and begged for my father's sake. I still didn't think it was right because you are still a child. But they set the date anyway. Then you ran away. I was glad, but I was worried about you. Yesterday evening, your Auntie Three came and said you were captured by bandits but were okay. She also delivered a message from your Ah Mah asking that we hold the wedding today, if it was okay with us. So you wouldn't try to run away or give us trouble again, your Ah Mah suggested that the ceremony be as simple as possible, as long as you offered tea.

"My mother agreed. She also postponed the banquet, since Father is so sick. I knew your Ah Mah wouldn't let you off the hook, and I didn't want you to run around again and get hurt. So, for my father's sake also, I finally agreed."

I said quietly, "Thank you for your concern. But I have ruined everything."

"What do you mean?"

"In the end, I did want to get married."

"But I thought . . . ?"

"I made a deal with Auntie Three. She said she would let me go back to see my Ah Pau if I cooperated. That's the *only* reason I agreed to get married. But I messed up. I thought your father was the groom. Now Auntie Three has something to hold against me and will not let me see my Ah Pau. She is very sick." I started to weep.

"Oh, I see. . . . Don't worry. I'll try to help you."

"Go back to my Ah Pau?" I questioned, not really sure if I should believe him.

"Is it what you really want to do?"

"Yes, but my Ah Mah will send Ah Fu or someone to catch me again."

"No, she won't."

"How can you be sure?"

"Well, we haven't offered tea to my parents and uncles and aunties, which means you haven't been accepted yet as a member of the Lo family. But . . . since your family has already accepted our bride price and you are my fiancée, the Lo family can now have say-so over you instead of your Ah Mah. I don't know why your Auntie Three promised to let you go back."

"Do you mean that the Lo family has control over me?" I really didn't quite understand.

"You could say that. But . . ." he continued, in a low voice, "I will help you return to Tai Kong. Just keep this between you and me."

"You're not trying to trick me?"

"Why would I trick you? I wasn't supposed to come in here, but I knew something was wrong and that's why I came here secretly to talk with you."

"Will you swear that you are telling me the truth?"

"You really want me to?"

"Yes."

He stuck up three fingers and swore: "On top of me is the heaven god, below me is the earth god. I, Lo Sing, am in the middle. If I ever try to trick Yeung Ying, I will be punished by the heaven god and the earth god. Do you believe me now?"

I was satisfied.

"Good. I'm going to talk with my mother. I think the cook will bring you food pretty soon. Why don't you change into regular clothes so you'll feel more comfortable?"

He opened the wardrobe and took out a red outfit that matched my embroidered shoes. I wondered how the clothes got in there. They were supposed to be in Ah Mah's wicker suitcase in the sedan chair. Ah Mah had told me to take the clothes with me because they belonged to me. No wonder she had said that. I was so naive. I didn't have any doubt that she had planned for Auntie Three and Ah Fu to stop me on the way. No wonder Auntie Three said that Ah Mah was a sly old fox.

Lo Sing helped me get up from the floor and shook his head when I winced in pain, disgusted at the way his relatives had treated me. He said he would ask my maid to massage *teet da jow* on my back. I told him that the pain was nothing if I could just go back to Ah Pau. He wanted me to promise him if my back didn't feel better, I wouldn't delay getting some treatment. Then he said he was going to ask someone to get water for me to wash. There was a lacquered screen in the room for changing. It was decorated with inlays of mother-of-pearl. I told him that I could get water myself.

He said, "Remember, you are the fiancée of the son of one of the wealthiest families in Ling Dong. You *have* to be served." Then he headed for the door by the bed and gently closed it behind him. I didn't run out after him. I believed he was really trying to help me.

Chapter 16

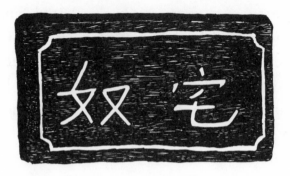

Someone knocked lightly on that same door while I was changing.

"Who is it?"

"It is Ah Ping, Miss Ying's maid," said a girl's voice. It was funny to hear that. I told her to come in. She was a pale, skinny girl with a long braid, carrying a washbasin in front of her. She looked younger than me, and appeared shy.

She carefully put the washbasin on the washstand beside the bed and bowed to me before she retreated. I felt even funnier about someone bowing to me.

I used a wet cloth to wash off the makeup. Then Ah Ping returned with a bowl of steaming noodles and tea on a fancy, lacquered tray. Again, very humbly, she carried the washbasin with her and bowed to me before she left.

I was ready to eat, but Lo Sing knocked and then came in from the front door. He gently closed the door behind him, looking deeply worried. I was very anxious to find out about his talk with his mother. He said, shaking his head, "My mother has finally accepted the fact that my father will die very soon. So there's no rush for the ceremony. But—" he shook his head, "there's the problem of the old custom."

"What do you mean?"

"My mother is very fond of you. She said since our birth dates are so well matched and our families' social levels are about the same, she plans to go ahead and raise you here like other families do with their child brides, rather than let you go back to your Ah Pau and such a hard life."

"What? They can't do that to me!"

"I told her that you are very homesick. Mother couldn't make up her mind because of my father. She said she would talk to my aunt."

"Which one?"

"Mrs. Tong."

"She's nice."

"But she hardly ever changes her mind once her mind is made up. The problem is that Mother always listens to my aunt because she is older and wiser."

"What are we going to do?"

"I don't know. But don't worry, I'll—"

Someone knocked on the side door rapidly. "Is Master Lo inside?"

"Yes," Lo Sing walked toward the door and opened it. "What's wrong?"

It was Ah Ping, looking anxious. "Go! Go see Mr. Lo, hurry."

"I'll be back," Lo Sing said to me, rushing out. Ah Ping followed him. I was left alone in the bride's room with the bowl of noodles untouched.

I don't know how long I waited. The sky did not seem as bright as earlier. My stomach was growling, but I still didn't feel like eating the noodles. Again, someone knocked on the front door of the room. I went to open it. It was Mrs. Tong. Seeing her, I immediately felt uneasy.

"Your future father-in-law has taken a turn for the worse," she said solemnly after she sat down. Her hair was done up in a shiny bun shaped like a butterfly at the back of her head. "All the Lo family members are at his bedside. We cannot hold the wedding ceremony while he is in such grave danger of passing away. So you can go back to Tai Kong tomorrow for the time being."

"Oh, thank you. Thank you, Mrs. Tong." I couldn't believe my ears.

"Don't thank me. Thank your fiancé. He cares very much about you, even with his father at death's door."

"Can I see him?"

"It's not the right time now. Lo Sing has already asked someone to get the sedan chair ready, and has engaged a sampan for you. Early tomorrow morning, the sedan bearers will escort you to Tai Kong.

"Where is the *dai kum?*"

"Well, she already left."

"Can the sedan bearers be trusted?"

"Of course. They have worked for the Lo family since even before Lo Sing was born. Your maid, Ah Ping, will accompany you, too. Then she will return immediately with the bearers. We'll need extra help here." She noticed the bowl of noodles was untouched and said, "Go ahead and eat the noodles. You are so skinny, you need to put food in your stomach to make yourself healthy." She got up from the chair, ready to leave. "And go to sleep soon. You will have a long day tomorrow," she added.

I thanked her. After she left, I devoured the cold, soggy noodles in no time! Ah Ping brought me a big basin of warm water, so I could take a sponge bath inside the room. I used the wooden chamber pot next to the bed rather than having to go to the outhouse. After that, the sky was almost dark, so Ah Ping prepared the mosquito net for me and I lay down on that big, fancy bride's bed. My back felt much better when I was lying down.

Very early the next morning, after breakfast in my room, Ah Ping helped me carry my few belongings, while Mrs. Tong accompanied me to say good-bye to the family. It was a big house. After turning down a couple of corridors, we entered the living room. There were only a few older people there, all looking very sad. Mr. Lo looked lifeless. He was lying on a makeshift bed. Lo Sing, who looked exhausted, knelt next to his father. He looked up at me. I just nodded at him, not knowing what to say.

"Say good-bye to Mr. and Mrs. Lo, Uncles, and Aunties," Mrs. Tong reminded me.

I said timidly, "Mr. Lo, Mrs. Lo, Uncles and Aunties, sorry I have to go now."

Mr. Lo didn't give any response. Mrs. Lo, whose hair was also in a bun shaped like a butterfly, looked completely drained. She sat in a chair next to her husband and gently said to him, "Ying said good-bye to you." But he still did not respond. Then she turned to me and said kindly, "This is your home now. Write to me whenever you want to come back, and I'll send someone to escort you."

I didn't know how to answer her because of the secret between Lo Sing and me. Lo Sing gave me a signal with his eyes, and I said, "I will."

She and the others instructed me to be careful on the journey, and Mrs. Tong told me that they had written to Ah Mah explaining what had happened. I wanted to thank Lo Sing, but not with other people around. So I just nodded at him without saying a word.

It was the first time I had really looked at the surroundings of the mansion, which consisted of several wings. A brick wall about eight feet high enclosed the property, with a flower garden in the front. Mrs. Tong escorted me on the red brick path lined with neatly trimmed bushes. Two man-made stone mountains with small bamboo plants growing out of them stood in the middle of water fountains on either side of the path. Water dripped down from the mountains and created a tinkling sound. I wanted to tell Mrs. Tong how beautiful the garden was, but I didn't. I hurriedly followed her toward the sliding wooden gate, afraid that she would change her mind and not let me go.

The wooden gate was already open. A shiny new

dark-red sedan chair and two bearers were waiting for me. I felt very relieved after I stepped through the gate. Over the gate was a black wooden plaque, with bright gold Chinese characters saying LO FAMILY. On either side of the gate hung red paper banners topped by round red paper lanterns, on which was written the character for DOUBLE HAPPINESS. These were decorations that families always hung at the time of a wedding.

I had wanted to thank Lo Sing. But I hastily walked toward the sedan chair where Ah Ping had already put my belongings. Mrs. Tong instructed Ah Ping to take good care of me on the journey, and she told me that she would see me back in Tai Kong. My heart was thumping. I feared Mrs. Tong would change her mind at the very last minute. But the sedan bearers raised up the chair and began to move. I felt like looking back at the mansion, hoping Lo Sing would come out, but I told myself not to.

Ah Ping, holding the food that we would eat on the journey as well as her belongings wrapped in a black kerchief, walked beside the sedan chair, just the way Ah Choi had. As the sedan chair turned into another narrow street, Ah Ping informed me, "Master Lo is coming!" I turned to look back, and saw Lo Sing running toward us.

The bearers slowed down and stopped. Pretty soon Lo Sing caught up with us and said breathlessly, "Sorry I can't accompany you to Tai Kong, but I am glad you are able to go back home. Here is my address at school. Write to me and let me know how everything is going."

"I don't know how to thank you, Lo Sing. I will never forget what you did."

"You don't need to mention it," he said in true humility. "I have to go back now."

I waved at him and he waved back. I watched him disappear as he turned the corner into another street. Then I read his note, evidently written in a hurry. It said, "At the right time and right moment, I will convince my mother to cancel the engagement. So don't worry and take care of yourself. Here is my address."

I felt my eyes moisten. How I wished that all the people around me were as nice as he was. "Thank you, Lo Sing," I whispered, and sunk into the sedan chair, still gripping the note tightly.

Chapter 17

We got to Tai Kong very late the same day. I cried when I saw my Ah Pau, because she was still alive! Ah Pau cried, too. Ah Pau was overjoyed to see me and held my hands for a long time, like she wouldn't let me go ever again. She said she had been crying every day since I had left, and that she regretted agreeing to lie to me about Ah Mah's sickness. I told Ah Pau I would forgive her and I would never be mad at her. She said Ah Mei and her mother had helped her out while I was gone. But she was feeling much better now. In fact, her condition was not as critical as Auntie Three had claimed. I realized that Auntie Three couldn't have known how Ah Pau was and that she was using Ah Pau's illness to control me.

After I told Ah Pau about all my ordeals during those

several days, she instructed me never to mention anything about it to anybody. She feared that I would have trouble finding a husband later on if people knew I had once been engaged. She said I had met a noble man, Lo Sing, and told me to write a letter to him and to Ah Mah, letting them know that I was safely home. Well, I only wrote to Lo Sing—I refused to write to Ah Mah. I was still angry about the way she had tricked me.

Soon after I returned home, Uncle arrived from Canton by steamboat. He praised me for writing the letter to him about Ah Pau's illness. Ah Pau wasn't upset at me for writing behind her back. In fact, she was proud of me.

The day after uncle arrived, he took Ah Pau with him to Canton for treatment.

I went back to school and got busy catching up on the lessons I had missed. Ah Mei's family offered to let me stay with them while Ah Pau was gone. I didn't tell anyone about what had happened, not even Ah Mei. Later, Uncle wrote to say that Ah Pau had a kidney infection, but she was getting better. She would stay in Canton for about a month.

While Ah Pau was in Canton, Auntie and Kee returned from visiting Auntie's family. Auntie looked about the same. But Kee had grown skinnier and taller, fitting his nickname "Bamboo Pole" even better.

Mr. Lo died shortly after I returned to Tai Kong. During the one hundred days following the death of his father, Lo Sing was busy going back and forth between Ling Dong and Canton for the mourning ceremonies.

At the beginning of the summer holiday in July, Ah

Pau told me to visit Ah Mah, since we had been reconnected after being out of touch for years. I told Ah Pau that I didn't want to see Ah Mah again. Ah Pau lectured me by saying, "No matter how she treated you, she'll always be your Ah Mah because she's your father's mother."

Even though I didn't want to do it, I agreed that I would stay at Ah Mah's house for one night, but that was all. I was actually hoping to see the wild child, rather than Ah Mah. Kee and Ah Mei, who wanted a little adventure, accompanied me on the boat journey while Auntie kept Ah Pau company at home. Ah Mei carried a basket full of star fruit. The boat was old and much smaller than the one I had traveled in before. Ah Mei and I both got seasick. Ah Mei swore that she would not ride in that kind of boat again. I felt better after I got in the front to breathe the fresh air, and I kept looking straight ahead instead of sideways. Ah Mei did the same, and she stopped complaining. When we got to Lam Cheun, it was still light. I didn't know how to get to Ah Mah's house. But because her name was well known, we didn't have any problem finding directions.

Ah Choi opened the door.

"Ah Choi!" I greeted her. She looked at me as if she were seeing a ghost. She stammered, "Ah . . . ah . . ." and let us in. Then she retreated immediately to the kitchen.

After handing the basket of fruit to me, Kee and Ah Mei gaped at the huge house. I had a funny feeling when I entered the living room. Ah Mah was not there. Only Auntie Three sat on the daybed, knitting. Kee and Ah Mei followed me.

"Auntie Three!" I greeted her. I had completely for-given her for what she had done to me, because I thought she was just carrying out Ah Mah's orders. But like Ah Choi, she started mumbling something I didn't under-stand. Before I could ask her where Ah Mah was, she ran back to her room.

We heard a muffled crying sound. After listening care-fully, I found that it came from Ah Mah's room. I looked in to check. She was sitting on her bed, sobbing. I couldn't believe my eyes! Ah Mah, with all her money and power, was weeping! But then I noticed that her long braid was not formed into a nice bun like she usually wore; it hung limply on her chest. She looked like she hadn't gotten up all day. *She must really be sick this time*, I thought. I walked into her room, but Kee said he and Ah Mei would wait outside.

"Ah Mah," I greeted her.

She stopped crying and used her sleeves to dab at her eyes. "Ying! How did you get here? I didn't expect to see you."

"My cousins accompanied me here." I went out of the room and told Kee and Ah Mei to come in. They greeted Ah Mah, then politely retreated.

"Ah Pau told me to come see you," I said to Ah Mah, "and she sent her regards." I gave her the basket of fruit.

Her appearance was completely different. On my last visit she looked rich and delicate, yet acted mean and pow-erful. Now, she was an ordinary, sick, lonely old lady—fragile and plain-looking. Her face was pale, without any makeup or jewelry, except for the jade earrings and bangle, which looked too big for her wrist. She seemed pitiful. So I said in a soft voice, "Is anything wrong, Ah Mah?"

She burst into tears again. After a while, she said, "I'm just feeling sorry for myself. I don't have much time left. My only wish is to have my children here to see me go. But your Uncle Three died without any children of his own, and your parents work far away. They can't come back here easily. None of them is around, now. Your Ah Pau is much luckier than me."

I remembered Ah Pau telling me that the most pitiful time of a person's entire life was when he is old, sick, and alone. I felt sorry for her.

She continued. "I am glad you are here so I can talk to you. I realize I was harsh to you. I don't know why. Perhaps . . . perhaps I was still angry at your parents, especially your mother. They both insisted on letting you stay with your Ah Pau before they left for Hong Kong, rather than letting you stay with me. They said it was good for you because there were many cousins there around your age.

"You are the only close kin I have nearby, even though we are not as close as we should be. I cared about you the most because your parents were so far away." I noticed her eyes glittering with moisture under the light. "But, I was selfish. I wanted you to have your own family before I was gone, so I could go peacefully, without worrying about you. I didn't realize that you are not an ordinary eleven-year-old girl."

"It's in the past now, Ah Mah," I said. Seeing how pitiful she was, I completely forgave her for what she had done to me before.

"I am very touched. I have never known a grandchild who would take a risk for her grandmother like you did for your Ah Pau. I am glad I found you and am getting to know you." She held my hand and continued, "You have courage that I admire. That's why I granted your wish and let you go back to your Ah Pau."

"What did you say, Ah Mah?" I was confused. Auntie Three had told me that Ah Mah had tricked me.

As I started to ask her to explain, Ah Choi burst into the room and cried, "She's gone! She's gone!"

Chapter 18

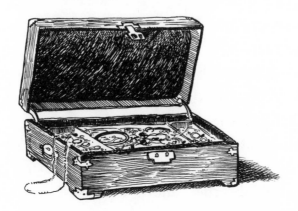

"Who's gone?"

Ah Choi abruptly dropped to the floor and bowed to Ah Mah, sobbing, "Mrs. Three and some of her belongings are gone. Please, please forgive this stupid maid. Please forgive my stupidity and confusion for not letting—"

"Stop crying and tell me what's going on!" Ah Mah ordered.

Ah Choi stopped crying, but was afraid to look up. "Mrs. Three said if I didn't do what she told me to do, she would kick me out of the house after Mrs. Yeung is gone. . . . I do not have any children and I do not have any family. I was afraid I wouldn't have any place to go when I am old. So I had to do what she told me to. Please, have mercy on me," she said, kowtowing.

"Tell me what she told you to do!" Ah Mah struggled to get up.

"Please have mercy. That day I was supposed to take Miss Ying back to Tai Kong, on the way to the ferry, Mrs. Three stopped us. I knew something wasn't right, but Ah Fu was there, too. He kept me from running to Miss Ying."

"Why was Ah Fu there?"

"I didn't know. I guess Mrs. Three had told him to help her."

What did that mean? Didn't Ah Mah send Ah Fu to get me on the day I got caught by the bandits? I said, "I got caught by the bandits because I was trying to flee from Ah Fu, too." Ah Mah looked at me, stunned. Then I told her what had happened that day.

"I knew there must be something going on when she asked Ah Fu to run errands for her!" Ah Mah said. Then she asked Ah Choi what Ah Fu did that day.

"He warned me not to say anything to you. I asked him what Mrs. Three would do to Miss Ying, and he said it was her big day."

Ah Mah slumped on her bed. She anxiously asked me, "Have you already offered tea to the parents?"

"Not quite," I said. Then I told her how I had agreed to get married for Auntie Three, but then struggled and disrupted the ceremony.

Ah Mah stared at Ah Choi, who was still pressing her forehead to the floor. She questioned Ah Choi, "That means they didn't get my letter and the returned bride price? What did you do with them?"

"I should die. That day when you gave me the letter,

I was ready to take it to the Lo family. But Mrs. Three came into the kitchen and told me to give it to her. I was afraid to disobey her, because she said she would be in charge of this house soon."

I remembered that on the day I returned to Ah Pau, Mrs. Tong told me Mrs. Lo had written a letter to Ah Mah explaining why I was returning to Ah Pau. So I asked, "Did you get Mrs. Lo's letter, Ah Mah?"

"What letter?"

Ah Choi bumped her head on the floor and cried, "Mrs. Three got it. She said all the letters addressed to you had to be turned over to her."

"How dare she! No wonder I haven't heard from the Lo family for quite a while. I thought they were still in mourning and that's why they had stopped communicating." She turned to Ah Choi and questioned, "How about the bride price?"

"Mrs. Three said she would handle it."

"What nerve! She must have used it to pay off her gambling debts!"

While I was still confused about Auntie Three, Ah Mah suddenly began breathing rapidly. I didn't know what to do, but Ah Choi hurriedly massaged Ah Mah's chest until her breathing returned to normal. Then she poured out some herbal tea from the insulated jar next to the bed for Ah Mah. Finally, she helped Ah Mah lie down.

"What about the bride price?" I asked. I was concerned.

"That's the problem." Ah Mah let out a sigh. "At least she's feeling guilty now. That's why she ran away. I am also concerned about how to find proof that I tried to cancel the marriage."

I didn't know what kind of proof she was talking about, until Ah Choi was still blaming herself, saying, "That's all my fault. If I hadn't given her the letter and the—"

"The letter!" I exclaimed. I thought about that day Ah Choi looked like she had been crying while Auntie Three crumpled up something red and white and threw it into the woodpile against the wall. Was that the letter? I hoped it was still there. It had been a few months ago. . . .

"Wait!" I said. I ran to the kitchen and quickly removed the firewood from the wall. But I couldn't find it. I dragged myself back to Ah Mah's room and said, "It's not there, Ah Mah. What should we do?"

"Well, the Lo family are decent people. They'll take my word for it. But the bride price . . . Auntie Three probably will return at least part of it."

Would she? And how about the rest? I was worried.

Ah Choi bowed her head to the floor again. Ah Mah said to her, "You have worked for me for many decades and you've always been very loyal to me and to the Yeung family. I forgive you for what you have done. Get off the floor."

"Thank you, thank you," Ah Choi said, crying. "Thank you for having mercy on this useless maid." She kowtowed to the floor, making three loud bumps.

Ah Mah was exhausted. She said, "I'm very tired," and closed her eyes.

While Ah Choi left the room half bowed over in humility, I held Ah Mah's hand and said, "I am sorry I was wrong about you, Ah Mah."

"I don't blame you," she said wearily, squeezing my hand. "I am feeling much better now. It feels so good to have my grandchild come to see me."

I gently helped her pull up the cover. She closed her eyes. I whispered, "I will be close by, Ah Mah." Then I left her room.

When I came out of Ah Mah's room, Kee and Ah Mei were sitting on the daybed, waiting for me. "How's your Ah Mah doing, Ying?" they both asked.

I simply said, "I will tell you later. She's feeling better now." Then I went to refresh myself. I stole a look at the storage room. There was no sign of the wild child. But I didn't feel sad. I thought he would be okay. He was young and tough, but my Ah Mah wasn't.

I wished I could spend a few days with Ah Mah, but there was no way to inform Ah Pau. Ah Pau would be very worried if we didn't go back when we had planned. So, after supper, Kee and Ah Mei went in to say good night to Ah Mah. I was very tired, but I wanted to spend more time with her, so I sat on the chair next to her bed. Most of the time, she slept. I stayed there until I was so sleepy that my head kept dropping down. Then I gently said good night to Ah Mah and slept in the living room where Ah Choi had fixed three pallets for us.

The next morning before we left, I held Ah Mah's hand and told her that I would return soon. I told her I would spend more time with her the next time I came.

She told me to give her regards to Ah Pau. She held my hands for a long time and seemed unwilling for me to go. I could barely contain my tears.

I didn't say anything for a long time after leaving Ah Mah's house.

Epilogue

Just as Ah Mah had predicted, Auntie Three sent someone to return a portion of the bride price that she hadn't spent. She said that she was just holding the bride price in the beginning, but she couldn't stand the temptation and finally used part of it to pay off her gambling debts. She said it was impossible for her to return the part she had stolen. She admitted that she had used Ah Fu to help her stop me from going back to Tai Kong. She wanted me to get married so she could inherit Ah Mah's big house.

Ah Mah forgave her because Auntie Three said she was going to quit gambling. Ah Mah told her she could come back, but Auntie Three said she didn't have the nerve to face Ah Mah and the other people in Lam

Cheun. She was ashamed of what she had done, and stayed in the town where her parents were. Ah Fu no longer worked as a day laborer for the Yeungs.

Lo Sing also wrote to tell me the engagement between him and me had been canceled: Ah Mah had requested it after I went to see her in July, and Lo Sing had convinced his mother. Ah Mah returned the title to the land and the portion of the bride price that Auntie Three hadn't used. I don't know what Ah Mah and Mrs. Lo arranged for the rest of it. So I was free! Ah Pau was very happy about it. However, Mrs. Lo was so fond of me that she wanted me to visit with them whenever I went to visit Ah Mah. But I didn't.

Ah Ping was no longer my maid, but she worked for Mrs. Lo because her parents had already sold Ah Ping to the Los.

In August, my Ah Mah became very ill. Kee accompanied me to Lam Cheun at once to see her. As soon as we arrived, I went to Ah Mah's bedside. I held her hand that day and the next. Even though she was dying, she still knew me, and she seemed at peace because I was there. I was sitting next to her when she just stopped breathing and left this world.

My parents couldn't come back in time for the funeral, so I was the one to lead the funeral procession, which was normally the oldest son's duty. In her will Ah Mah left the house to all her descendants, but she gave Ah Choi permission to stay there for the rest of her life.

I had not seen the wild child since the day I got caught by the bandits. One hundred days after Ah Mah's death, in November, I went back to Lam Cheun for the last funeral ceremony in her honor. In the late evening, I saw Ah Choi carrying a meal outside to the storage room. I discovered that she was feeding the wild child! At last I knew for sure why he hadn't been poisoned by Auntie Three.

I was glad that he was safe and had someone to take care of him. I had always wondered what happened to him on the day I was caught.

At home, our lives finally went back to normal. I was happy to be living with Ah Pau and her family again. I no longer envied the rich girls' fancy clothes. I was content with my plain, worn-out ones, because I was free to do anything I wanted. I was just an eleven-year-old girl again, and I didn't want to be anything else.

Glossary

Ah Mah   Grandmother (father's mother).

Ah Pau   Grandmother (mother's mother).

aiyah!   Chinese exclamation.

bok choy   A Chinese vegetable with long white stalks and green leaves.

bound feet   An old traditional Chinese custom in upper-class families. Young girls about six or seven years old had their feet bound to prevent their feet from growing to full size. The custom was established two thousand years ago and persisted until it was abandoned during the early years of the Chinese Republic, which followed the Ching Dynasty.

bride price   A gift that the groom's family offers the bride's family before they get married.

Canton   The biggest city in southeastern China, now known as Guangzhou.

Ching Dynasty   The last imperial dynasty in China, dated 1644–1911.

dai gut lai see   The Chinese equivalent of the expression "knock on wood."

dai kum   A woman hired by the bride's family to assist the bride during the wedding ceremony.

double happiness   The Chinese character symbolizing the joy of a wedding.

dowry   In Chinese custom, money or goods that the wife's family gives to the wife or couple at the time of marriage.

keepo   A long *tong cheong sam* a woman's fancy tunic.

kowtow   To kneel down and touch the forehead to the floor to show respect.

Kung Kung   Grandfather (father's father).

Kwun Yum   Chinese goddess of mercy.

mah-jongg   A game from China, which can be used for gambling, usually played by four persons with 144 tiles that are drawn and discarded until one player secures the winning hand.

meh dai   A cloth baby carrier used to carry a baby on someone's back.

see kung   A man who directs a funeral ceremony in China.

seen ji   A very precious hardwood. The trees grew very slowly, and the wood was very dense and hard. This kind of wood is no longer readily available.

seh yeuk   A laxative made from herbs.

Tai Kong   My town; its name is now Dagangzhen.

teet da jow   A kind of herbal medicine for bruises and sprains.

Tiger Balm   A medicinal ointment good for headaches and stomachaches.

tong cheong sam   A traditional Chinese tunic.

yuan   The Chinese unit of money: one hundred Chinese cents equals one *yuan*.